"Don't you want to hear about my fantasies?

"You know, the ones where I'm not so saintly?" Mattie continued playfully.

Brad stepped back slightly. "Mattie, this isn't a good idea."

She put the tea towel down on the kitchen counter and closed the distance between them. "I think this is the best idea either of us has ever had." And before he could protest further, she pressed her mouth to his.

For an instant he held back. Mattie could sense his struggle with his own stringent morals—morals that had kept him from her years ago. This time, however, he lost.

In a flash Brad went from passive to passionate. He pulled her to him, holding her tight in his arms— so tight she was having trouble catching her breath. She was trembling with need, wanting Brad now more than ever.

Suddenly, abruptly, Brad broke the kiss. Pressing his forehead to hers, he said, "Don't get me wrong, Sprout. You're tempting. But I didn't want to break your heart when you were eighteen, and I don't want to break it now." With that, he walked out of the room.

Mattie watched him leave, content knowing that he was as affected as she was. She'd have Brad Sumners in her bed. It was just a matter of time....

Dear Reader,

Who doesn't remember their high school crush?

You know the one…that boy you couldn't stop thinking about. The object of your adolescent affections. The star of your teenage fantasies.

If you're anything like Mattie Wilcox, you've never stopped wondering about the one that got away. Of course, in Mattie's case that boy—Brad Sumners—is the older brother of her best friend and roommate, Jessica.

When Brad, fresh from his divorce, returns to their little town to get advice about women from his sister, Mattie has to face those teenage fantasies head-on. To make matters worse, Jessica is sent on an impromptu business trip and she leaves Mattie in charge of healing Brad's broken heart.

If you enjoy reading about Brad and Mattie, look for Jessica's story, which will be out in 2005. If you'd like to hear more about Jessica's book and my other books, please visit my Web site, www.EmilyMcKay.com. You can write me at P.O. Box 163104, Austin, TX 78716-3104. I'd love to hear from you!

Emily McKay

Books by Emily McKay

HARLEQUIN TEMPTATION
912—BABY, BE MINE

EMILY McKAY

PERFECTLY SEXY

HARLEQUIN®

TORONTO • NEW YORK • LONDON
AMSTERDAM • PARIS • SYDNEY • HAMBURG
STOCKHOLM • ATHENS • TOKYO • MILAN • MADRID
PRAGUE • WARSAW • BUDAPEST • AUCKLAND

To my husband, Greg, for being the hero
of my life's story and for teaching me that
love should be fun as well as powerful.

ISBN 0-373-69176-9

PERFECTLY SEXY

1

BRAD SUMNERS—successful entrepreneur, former high school football quarterback, and all-around Greek God. Of all the things Mattie Wilcox could imagine him needing advice about, women was dead last on the list.

"Let me see if I've got this right." Mattie eyed her best friend and roommate speculatively. "Your brother needs advice and, since you're leaving town, I'm elected?"

Jessica Sumners tossed two suitcases on her bed. "Come on," she cajoled. "You and I have been best friends since the sixth grade. We practically grew up together. He thinks of you as a sister." She scooped the entire contents of one dresser drawer into her arms and then dumped it into one of the open bags.

Mattie raised her eyebrows at Jessica's uncharacteristic packing. Seeing Jessica—who was normally so calm and sophisticated—this rattled was a bit amusing, really. But who wouldn't be rattled under the circumstances? Packing for a nine-week trip in less than an hour would make anyone panicked. But Jessica? Jessica, who organized her wardrobe by color and planned her schedule up to six months in advance? Of course this had sent her into a tailspin.

Mattie gently nudged her friend into the chair by the bed. "Just sit down." Jessica started to stand back up. "Calm down. You're getting all...flitty on me."

"Flitty?" Jessica's voice rose several octaves. "Of course I'm flitty. They're sending me to Sweden for nine weeks and I've only got—" she snatched up her alarm clock and stared at it "—twenty minutes to pack. It's noon?" She shook the clock, tapping it against her palm as if to test that it was working properly. "Is this right?"

Mattie glanced at her own watch. "'Fraid so." Noticing the harried expression on Jessica's face, she continued, "It's okay. I'll help you pack. Just remember, it's Sweden. You've been begging your boss to send you abroad on business since you started working there."

Jessica sucked in a deep breath and visibly relaxed as she exhaled. "You're right. I just wish I had more time to prepare. And to help Brad. This just kills me. The first time my big brother asks for help and I can't be here to give it. Promise me you'll help him."

The distress in Jessica's sapphire eyes tugged at Mattie's heart. She answered without thinking. "Of course I will."

She would do whatever it took to help out, even though the thought of seeing Brad Sumners again after all these years made *her* feel all flitty. "I'll talk to Brad. I promise."

Something in her voice must have given her away, because Jessica frowned, then said, "Oh, Mattie, I didn't think. This is going to be awkward for you, isn't it? Because you were in love with him for all those years."

"Nonsense." She brushed aside her own needs with a wave of her hand. "That wasn't love. That was teenage hormones. Lusting after a hunky guy isn't the same thing as love. Doesn't matter how hot he is. I'll be fine."

Jessica studied her with a worried gaze. "You're sure?"

"Yes. Definitely. Go pack your hanging bag while I handle this suitcase."

While Jessica hurried off to her walk-in closet, Mattie sifted through the sleepwear and lingerie Jessica had dumped on the bed. She picked out only what Jessica would need for her trip, then carefully folded it and packed it into the open suitcase.

A few minutes later Jessica returned, holding a hanging bag in one hand and clutching an armful of casual clothes to her chest.

"Do you have room for these?"

As Mattie folded and packed the T-shirts, she asked, as casually as she could, "What kind of advice about women does he need? How to jump out of their way as they throw themselves at him? How to step over their prone bodies on the way out of his house every morning?"

"Mattie, be serious." Jessica slapped one suitcase closed and tugged on the zipper.

"I thought I was." When Jessica paused to glare at her, she held up her hands in a gesture of surrender. "Okay, okay. I'm serious."

"Besides, I don't think he needs advice about women so much as advice from a woman. You know, a woman's perception of things."

"But if he needs advice," Mattie asked, "why doesn't he just call you and get advice over the phone like a normal person?"

"Because this is Brad, remember? He's not a normal person. You know how he gets when he sets a goal for himself. He's totally focused. He's relentless. It's like he's got blinders on. Just like my team leader who was so focused on this project he worked himself into a case of pneumonia and had to be hospitalized this morning."

"And now you have to go to Sweden in his place." Mattie sighed, resting a hand dramatically over her heart. "Sweden in the summer. Rugged mountains, majestic fjords, and hunky Nordic men. If I wasn't so damn broke, I'd go with you."

Jessica paused and looked up. Then she dropped a handful of shoes into the open suitcase and rounded the corner of the bed, coming over to give Mattie a brief hug.

"I'll miss you."

Mattie returned the hug, squeezing her eyes shut against the prickling of tears. They'd been through Girl Scout cookie sales, high school calculus, and college term papers together.

A year ago, when Mattie had finally divorced her worthless husband, Jessica had been by her side lending support through it all. Jessica had given her a place to live, a shoulder to cry on, and at least a half-dozen boxes of Thin Mints. Aromatherapy for the broken-hearted, Jess had called them.

"I know the timing is horrible, but if we lose this account it could be my job." Jessica pulled back and smiled brightly. "And it's only nine weeks. Besides, they're paying me oodles of money for going on such short notice. And I happen to know a little quilt store that could use an investor."

"I've told you before. I'm not letting you give me money. It's bad enough that you don't let me pay more rent. I won't let you—"

Jessica waved aside the protest and crammed a few more items into the suitcase. "I wouldn't be giving it to you. I'd be making an investment. But we'll discuss that later. Besides, if you can handle this Brad crisis for me, I'll really owe you."

"You know, he may not want advice from me. We haven't seen each other for years. He probably doesn't even remember me."

"Trust me, he remembers you." Jessica zipped the last suitcase closed; then she picked up a suitcase in each hand and nodded toward the hanging bag. "Get that one, will you?"

Mattie groaned under the weight, following Jessica through the living room to the front door.

Jessica set the suitcase on the marble tile of the foyer then opened the door to watch for her taxi. "Brad's rearranged his schedule so he can work from here for a couple of weeks, so whatever advice he needs must be important. He never takes time off work, but I got the feeling he didn't want to be alone on his birthday. He just hasn't been the same since the divorce. Ginger broke his heart—the witch."

"The witch?" Mattie asked. "That's generous of you."

"Meee-ooow."

"Oh, was I being catty?" Mattie feigned surprise. "You know, I think that's the worst thing I've heard you say about your ex-sister-in-law."

"When Brad gets here, could you at least try to be sympathetic? He probably just wants a shoulder to cry on."

Mattie snorted in exaggerated disbelief. The Brad she knew cried on no one's shoulder. The Brad she knew didn't cry at all. "His junior year, a three-hundred-pound linebacker shattered his femur. He didn't shed a single tear. I can't imagine him crying over a broken heart. Certainly not to someone he hasn't seen in a decade."

Jessica shot her a wry look. "I was speaking metaphorically."

To lighten the mood, she added, "Okay, okay. I'll be here. I'll be sympathetic. I'll be like the sister he's never had."

The corner of Jessica's mouth twitched up in a smile. "He has a sister. Remember?"

"So I'll be like the sister he has, but who's in Sweden."

"Just be sympathetic." Outside, a car honked. "That's my ride."

Less than a minute later, Mattie stood alone in the doorway watching Jessica's taxi disappear down the road. She gave herself exactly one minute of feeling lonely and abandoned before shutting the front door and heading back to Jessica's room. The evidence of Jessica's hurried packing lay strewn across the cream cotton duvet. Mattie quickly rehung the clothes and returned the shoes to their cubbyholes in the closet. She paused while folding one of Jessica's camisoles. The scent of Jessica's lavender lingerie detergent wafted through the air.

Mattie sighed, squelching her jealousy.

Everybody had a different destiny. You had to settle for the cards fate handed you, even if you didn't necessarily like them. That's just the way the world worked. It was all part of the great cosmic poker game.

Jessica's cards held trips to Sweden, a well-paying job, and lavender-scented soap. Her own cards?

Her cards held a quilt shop inherited from her grandma, scraps of money left at the end of the month, and whatever detergent happened to be on sale.

Fortunately they also held great friends, fun employees, and the rare bottle of Woolite. All in all, not so bad.

However that didn't mean she wanted Brad Sumners showing up in her poker hand anytime soon. After dropping the camisole into the drawer, she slid it shut. She had more important things to be thinking about. To start with, finding a way for A Stitch in Time to make more money. She had employees who depended on her for their living. She had promises she'd made to her grandmother.

Her own desires, needs and adolescent fantasies

were nothing compared to that. Dealing with Brad would be a snap.

She hoped.

"Everyone has stupid high school crushes," she told herself. "It's part of life."

She ignored the voice in her head that reminded her that her stupid crush had started in the sixth grade and lasted all the way through college and a good part of her marriage. Her stupid crush on Brad had sabotaged every romantic relationship she'd ever had.

MATTIE PULLED the elastic scrunchie out of her hair, then scraped her fingernails over her scalp.

"Brad means nothing to you now." Hours later, and she was still trying to convince herself.

She pulled her clothes off, wadding them into a ball and shooting them across her bedroom into the laundry basket.

She crossed the hall to the bathroom continuing her monologue while she waited for the water to run hot.

"I mean it, too. You're not fifteen anymore. You're past that." She braced one hand on the tile wall and thrust the other under the stream of steamy water. Perfect.

"He'll visit. You'll be sympathetic. That's it."

As she stepped into the shower, she noticed the bottle of Fresh Freesia shower gel. Jess was always leaving fancy gels and shampoos in here for her.

Mattie started to reach for her own bar of Ivory, like she always did, but paused. What would it hurt? Surely one fresh freesia shower wouldn't spoil her forever. As she flipped open the cap and inhaled the light floral scent, she found herself humming "Love is a Battlefield."

By the time she stepped out of the shower a few minutes later, she'd graduated from humming to belting it out at the top of her lungs. She paused only long enough to wrap her hair in a towel. Grabbing another towel off the rack, she headed for her bedroom.

It wasn't until she opened the bathroom door that she heard the phone ringing. For a brief second, she contemplated letting the machine get it, but Jessica might have forgotten something.

After trotting down the hallway to the kitchen, she snatched up the phone and was about to punch the talk button when she noticed the dog prints.

A trail of large, muddy paw prints led across Jessica's plush cream carpet, over the snowy tile floor and toward the sliding-glass door to the backyard.

Which was really odd, considering she didn't have a dog.

Still holding the phone, she followed the trail to the back door and looked out. Sure enough, there sat a large, honey-colored Lab, and…a man, crouching just in front of the dog, wrestling for control of a paw.

Her heart leaped. Brad.

There. In her backyard—well, Jessica's backyard. With a dog.

The phone in her hand gave one last shrill ring before being cut off. She blinked at the handset for a second, then realized the machine had picked up the call. Quickly she punched the talk button.

"Hello?"

"Oh...hi." It was Jessica. "I was about to leave a message. I thought I'd missed you."

Mattie didn't take her eyes off Brad as she answered. "I was just getting out of the shower." She couldn't help noticing a thousand little details about him: the way his blond hair—now darker than it had been the last time she'd seen him in person—still gleamed in the sun. The way the white cotton of his oxford shirt stretched taut across his unbelievably wide shoulders. The way his crisp khakis molded his lean hips and firm buttocks.

"I'm glad I caught you. I forgot to tell you Brad has a key."

"Oh. Yeah." Just then the dog looked up and noticed her. The glass door separating them barely muffled the noise as the dog barked at her. "That makes sense."

Brad stiffened then glanced over his shoulder. A second passed. Then he stood and turned to face her.

The instant his eyes met hers, every cell in her body seemed to shake itself awake. In the years since she'd last seen him she'd convinced herself his eyes weren't as spectacularly blue as she remembered. She'd convinced herself no one had eyes the color of the ocean's depths. She'd been wrong.

Mattie felt a familiar jolt of adrenaline. Entranced by his gaze, a second passed before Jessica's voice intruded over her own thundering heartbeat. "...you okay? You sound really strange."

"Sorry," she mumbled. Try as she might, she couldn't seem to take her eyes off Brad. "I'm just...um..." Finally she tore her eyes away from him and shook her head to clear it. "It's just that I'm dripping on the floor."

And that's when she remembered she was wearing only a towel.

2

THERE WAS A NAKED WOMAN in his sister's living room.

Nearly naked, anyway. She wore only a bright yellow towel wrapped sarong-style around her torso and a blue towel twined like a turban on her head. Other than that, she was completely naked. Gloriously naked.

She was a tiny little thing—small enough that her cheek could rest right against his heart—but he didn't, not even for a minute, mistake her for anything other than a full-grown woman. Though slender, she had curves in all the right places. That yellow towel hid little, and accentuated everything else. The bare length of her thighs, the swell of her hips, the arch of her breasts, the delicate jut of her collarbone.

He swallowed, trying to ease the sudden dryness in his mouth. She was obviously just out of the shower and he was instantly aware that her skin would still be moist and that droplets of water would pool at the hollow of her throat.

His gaze slipped up to her eyes. They widened, mirroring his own surprise. Her lips parted, and he could have sworn he heard her gasp, which he knew wasn't possible. A good ten feet—not to mention the sliding-glass doors—separated them. She frowned, then spun around and hurried across the living room and out of his view.

For a moment, he just stood there, staring at the spot where she'd been. He shook his head to clear it, then ran a hand down his face as if to scrub away his haziness.

Damn. The months of celibacy since Ginger left him had taken more of a toll than he'd realized.

He had no idea who this woman was. In his earlier haste to get his rambunctious golden Lab, Madison, through the house and out into the backyard, he'd been too preoccupied to notice anything and he'd probably left the front door unlocked. This could be some stranger who'd wandered in off the street. Some crazy person, for all he knew. Scenes from half a dozen thrillers flashed through his mind. He shoved them aside.

Great. Now he was paranoid.

Trying to muster a normal amount of brotherly indignation, he looked down at Maddie.

"Who the hell was that?"

Maddie barked once then rushed around him to paw at the door as if saying *I don't know. Let's go find out.* When he didn't move, Maddie looked over her shoulder and barked at him.

"Yeah, I guess you're right," he told her. "But you're going to have to stay outside until I can finish cleaning those paws."

Brad stopped, notching his head to the side. Now he was talking to his dog. Really at the top of his game, wasn't he?

He stepped into his sister's living room, blocking the door with his foot so Maddie couldn't follow. Had Jessica ever mentioned having a roommate? He didn't think so. But the past couple of months he'd been distracted and for weeks now, he'd been swamped trying to clear his schedule so he could take time off. For all he knew, she'd told him the seven dwarfs had moved in and he just hadn't been paying attention.

He headed down the short hall that led to the bedrooms, pausing only to wince at the screech of dog claws against glass. Only one door was closed. Figuring she had to be behind that closed door, he knocked.

"Go away, Brad."

He frowned. *She knew him?*

That was...odd.

He raised his hand, paused for a second, then knocked again. "Excuse me, miss, but—"

The door swung open. His beautiful terry-wrapped mystery woman was wrapped now in jeans and a UCLA sweatshirt. Her damp, finger-combed hair fell just to her jawline. The bulky clothes didn't lessen her impact on him. Her nearly naked image was still too fresh in his mind. Yet, in the seconds it took him to study her delicate heart-shaped face and her now-loose hair, he realized his mystery woman wasn't such a mystery after all.

"Mattie?"

Eyes the color of summer moss narrowed. "Miss?"

"Mattie Wilcox?" he repeated. *This* was the girl he'd spent most of his senior year lusting after? "Sprout?"

Her eyes narrowed to slits and she ignored the affectionate nickname he'd given her so long ago. "You didn't even recognize me." She propped her hands on her hips and tapped her toe. "Did you?"

His heart stuttered. All that glorious naked flesh belonged to Mattie Wilcox? He'd spent the better part of his senior year wondering about the body she kept hidden beneath her tomboy clothes. Back in high school, he would have killed to see her dressed only in a towel.

Heat flooded his body. As he struggled to make sense of this information, everything he believed about beautiful women rolled over in his mind.

Playboy Bunnies had bodies like that. Women on *Baywatch* had bodies like that. Childhood friends who'd been the object of innocent crushes were not supposed to have bodies like that.

And he sure as hell wasn't supposed to go rock hard at the sight of them.

He forced his attention back to her face. "I..." He exhaled, frustrated by his sudden inability to compose a sentence. "No, I didn't." Her brow furrowed and he quickly tried to repair the damage. "But I've never seen you in a towel before."

The furrow transformed into an all-out frown. He took a step forward, only to have her slam the door inches from his nose. He winced.

For a minute he just stared at the closed door. Then, shaking his head in disbelief, he turned and made his way back down the hall.

The sexy towel-wrapped mystery woman was Mattie Wilcox? Why hadn't he recognized her?

They'd grown up together, for goodness' sake.

Of course, he hadn't seen her in...jeez, he didn't know when he'd last seen Mattie Wilcox.

Brad crossed to the cream-colored sofa. He sank to the edge of the plush cushion and propped his elbows on his knees. He sighed, rubbing his forehead with the heels of his hands.

More and more, it seemed Ginger had been right— he just didn't know crap about women.

"Your dog wants in."

Brad jerked his head up and turned to look at her. He shook his head in bemusement as he studied her. Sprout. His little Sprout, all grown up. Well, not grown *up*, as much as grown...*out*.

She cleared her throat. He cringed, forcing his eyes back to her face. Ogling a naked stranger was one thing. Ogling Sprout was another. Growing up, she'd been like a sister to him. Most of the time.

Her father had been his high school football coach. Coach Wilcox had wisely recognized the growing attraction between his daughter and his star football player. When Coach pulled Brad aside and insisted he stay away from Mattie, Brad had resented the interference.

But there was no other man in the world he respected as much as Coach Wilcox—not even his own father—and so he'd kept his distance. Forced himself to think of her as a kid sister. As Sprout.

Safely out of reach. Beyond temptation.

But she was all grown up now. No longer just Sprout. Nothing like a kid sister. And very much within reach. Something he was excruciatingly aware of as she walked past him toward the back door and her scent washed over him. She smelled like flowers. And something else as well. Something uniquely her.

Before he could say anything, she slid the door open just enough to grab the dog's collar. The dog tried to bound forward with a yip, but Mattie held tight, refusing to allow movement beyond the little floor mat.

"Sit," she commanded. Amazingly the dog sat. Over her shoulder, Mattie asked, "Do you have a towel or something?"

He'd left the towel he'd been using in the backyard. Since his dog now blocked the back door, Brad grabbed a dish towel from the kitchen table and handed it to her.

She reached for a paw, but before she could grab it, the dog stood. "Sit," she said again. This time, however, the dog didn't. "What's her name?" she asked Brad, not meeting his gaze.

"Maddie."

"What?" When he didn't respond, she looked over her shoulder. "What?"

"I, um...that's the dog's name."

"Excuse me?"

"Her name—" he pointed to the dog "—is Maddie."

She narrowed her eyes. "I guess that explains why you didn't recognize me. You were expecting someone...furrier."

When he realized what she meant, he winced.

He hadn't intended to insult her by naming his dog after her. For that matter, he hadn't intended to name his dog after her in the first place. Had he?

Had naming his dog Maddie been a subconscious attempt to reconnect with the real Mattie? Boy, that seemed pathetic. And he hadn't even gotten the spelling right.

"Maddie is short for Madison. Not Matilda," he said wryly.

Her mouth formed a little O of surprise. The movement brought his attention to her lips. God, no one off-limits should have lips that lush.

Before he had a chance to say anything more, a blush crept up her neck and she jerked her attention back to the dog. She ducked her head and a curtain of damp hair fell across her face, blocking his view of her cheek. The movement bared the back of her neck—slender, pale, vulnerable.

Brad squeezed his eyes closed against the sight. He inhaled and once again her scent hit him. She smelled fresh and clean, yet feminine. Like flowers. The ones that his grandmother had grown in her garden back when he was a kid. Those flowers always smelled like home to him. Combined with Mattie's scent, that smell transported him back to a simpler time and flooded him with memories of warm summer days spent in Mattie's backyard.

"You smell good," he murmured. His eyes shot open as he realized he'd said the words aloud as well as thought them.

Her back stiffened. She didn't look up. "Thank you." Wrestling for control of another paw, she added, "It's Jessica's. The scented soap, I mean."

He didn't bother to explain that he hadn't meant the

soap at all. He'd meant her. But she didn't need to know that.

Instead he said, "I'm sorry I didn't recognize you. I was expecting an empty house. Not you walking around—"

She didn't give him a chance to finish the thought. "I was expecting privacy in my own home."

"Your home?"

"Yes, I live here. I've been renting a room from Jessica for almost a year now." She moved on to the next paw. "So, yes, this is my home. At least until Jessica gets back. I'm probably going to find something else then."

"Back?"

"From Sweden." She paused to look up at him. In the instant before she looked back down, he thought he saw a flash of appreciation in her gaze. Only the barest hint of pink tinged her cheeks. Was she blushing because she had to rent a room from Jessica or because he'd caught her checking him out? "She left today."

"Jess is in Sweden?"

Nodding, she redoubled her efforts. "Yes. For nine weeks. It was a last-minute thing. She tried to call you, but couldn't get through."

The second Mattie loosened her hold on the dog's collar, Madison bounded forward. All gangly legs and massive paws, she lurched across the room in the direction of the front door before changing her mind and heading down the hall.

Mattie watched Brad's dog disappear without comment. She smiled as she stood and handed him the now-filthy towel. "I'll let you take care of this. Laundry room's that way," she said, pointing down the hall.

He stared down at the cloth, absently rubbing his thumb across the grit. Finally he repeated, "She's in Sweden?"

"Yep."

"For nine weeks?"

"Yep."

Nine weeks?

He had just two weeks before he had to be back in the Bay Area. Since his birthday fell toward the end of those two weeks—and since the thought of spending his first birthday since the divorce alone depressed him even more than the divorce had—he'd hoped to spend those weeks with Jess.

He hadn't seen her enough in the past couple of years and he didn't like the thought of the one family member he actually cared about drifting out of his life. Besides, he wanted her perspective on his divorce. He wanted to know if he was really the asshole Ginger said he was.

Almost as if she'd read his mind, Mattie chimed in. "Look, Brad, she told me you need advice about women." As she spoke, she started moving toward the front door. "And don't worry. I've got you covered on that front. Just not today. Come back tomorrow. We'll talk about it then."

She opened the door to show him out, but he didn't move.

Something in her expression brought to mind the first time he'd ever seen her. It was the summer he was about thirteen, if he remembered right. He'd been walking home from a friend's house. He turned the corner onto his block to find a U-Haul truck in front of one of the houses and this frail little girl sitting out on the curb, hands fisted on her knees, cheek resting on her hands, watching him as he walked toward her. She looked lost and broken. She'd flinched when he'd said hello as he walked by.

The instinct to protect her had been so strong, that night after dinner he'd pulled his sister aside and ordered her to go down the block and introduce herself to the girl. He'd wanted to help her, and giving her a friend was the only way he'd known how.

Until today, he'd never seen Mattie without thinking of that frail child, and it didn't matter that the frail child had quickly grown into a spunky tomboy with a sassy mouth.

But she was no longer the frail child or the spunky tomboy. She was all woman, with a woman's body and, if the interested spark in her eyes was any indication, a woman's appetites as well.

Surely there was a statute of limitations on warnings issued by overprotective fathers.

He was surprised to feel a smile forming on his face. The glint of suspicion in Mattie's eyes only added to his amusement.

"Come back tomorrow?" he asked. "Actually, I was hoping to stay here."

"YOU'RE NOT STAYING HERE."

"Why not?" He crossed to the kitchen sink and rinsed his hands. "Jess invited me months ago."

From the corner of her eye, Mattie saw Brad's dog plod back into the room. Nose to the ground, the dog worked her way across the carpet toward the kitchen. Jessica would have a fit if she saw the paw prints Madison had already left. All the more reason to boot Brad out.

"She may have invited you," Mattie pointed out, "but she's in Sweden now."

"Then I guess I'm staying with you." Brad's mouth twitched upward in the barest hint of a smile.

He might as well have sucker-punched her. At eighteen, he'd been handsome—focused and intense. But, dear God, at thirty-two he was devastating. He'd grown into his features. His square jaw and jutting chin had always seemed too big for the rest of his face. Now he'd filled out. It softened him, just enough to lend his smile the force of a professional kickboxer.

As if he knew he'd weakened her with the first blow and was now moving in for the final strike, he sauntered back to the living room, stopping mere inches from where she stood.

"What do you say? Wanna be roommates?"

Her stomach clenched in response, either to his smile or his words, she wasn't quite sure which. And, frankly, it didn't matter. Spending a couple of hours being sympathetic over dinner was one thing. This was something else entirely. The last thing she needed right now was for Brad to trample her heart like a herd of stampeding elephants.

Not that she was planning on letting him within stampeding range of her heart. Nope, not even for a minute.

But, just to be on the safe side, it was probably best if she kept him out of range of her body as well as her heart.

"No." Her response came out weaker than she'd hoped, so she cleared her throat and tried again. "Absolutely not. You can't stay with me."

"Come on, Mattie. Where else am I going to stay?"

"I don't care. Get a hotel room like anyone else would."

Madison made another pass of the living room floor and as she neared Brad, he reached out and snagged her collar. "There aren't any hotels in town that'll take Maddie. I checked."

"This is a resort town. You can't throw a cell phone without hitting an inn or a B and B. Surely one of them takes dogs."

"Not over fifty pounds."

"Well, you're rich. Bribe someone."

"I tried that. It earned me a half-hour lecture about how my generation has no respect for the past."

"Mrs. Higgins at the Cliffhouse?"

"How'd you guess?"

Mattie threw up her hands in exasperation. "I said bribe *someone*, I didn't say bribe the president of the Historical Preservation Society." She reached for Maddie's collar and began pulling the dog toward the door. To her surprise, Brad let himself be pulled along with her. "Go try someone else—someone who doesn't run the most exclusive inn in the county."

"Mattie, just let me stay here. It's only a week. Two at most. Madison and I won't get in your way. We promise."

"Won't get in my way, huh?" She pointed to the paw prints marring the cream carpet. "We both know Jessica's going to freak out when she sees these muddy prints."

"I'll pay to have the carpets cleaned."

"The best steam cleaner in the world may not get out this mess."

"Then I'll buy all new carpets." A slow, broad smile spread across his face. "I promise we'll behave."

Her stomach flipped over. He'd behave? If only she could get her hormones to make the same promise.

Besides, she knew that smile. That was his charming smile. He never smiled like that unless he wanted something.

"No. And that's final."

"It's just a couple of weeks."

"A couple of weeks? I thought it was one week."

He ducked his head, seemingly reluctant to continue. "Look, the house Ginger and I lived in just sold. I had to be out of there by this morning, but I can't move into the new condo for a couple of weeks. If I stay with you, I can work from here until then and I won't have to board Maddie."

He raised his head, pinning her with a serious look. Then he said the one thing sure to rip out her heart. "Come on, Mattie. I need you."

As if sensing her imminent surrender, he continued pleading. "Come on, Sprout, let us stay. You know you're not going to turn away someone in need."

Her hand clenched on the doorknob. He'd called her Sprout again. No one called her Sprout anymore. That had to stop.

She squeezed her eyes shut, remembering her promise to Jessica. She'd said she would help him. She couldn't let Jess down. More importantly, she couldn't let herself down. Brad had the power to hurt that lovesick girl, but she wasn't that girl anymore.

Besides, how hard could it be? As long as she kept things light and playful, he'd never know he still turned her insides to absolute mush. As long as she held him at arm's length, she would prove to herself—once and for all—that he held no power over her.

"One night. You can stay here tonight, but first thing in the morning I want you looking for another place." The smile he flashed her sent a rush of heat pounding through her body. Damn him.

Light and playful, she ordered herself. Keep it light and playful. "Oh, and while you're here, stop calling the dog Maddie."

For a second he stared at her in confusion—as if he couldn't imagine why she wouldn't want to share names with a dog—then he smiled. "Whatever you say, Sprout."

"And stop calling me that," she growled.

Okay, so she needed a little more work on the light and playful thing.

Make that a lot more work.

3

A FEW HOURS LATER, Brad found Mattie in the backyard, sprawled in a lounger by the pool, an open bottle of Fat Tire Amber Ale resting on the table beside her chair. In her hands, she held a worn deck of playing cards, the familiar blue-and-white pattern faded with time and use, and she shuffled them from one hand to the other. She paused and looked up when he approached, then tapped the stack against her palm.

She still wore jeans, but she'd lost the shoes and traded the UCLA sweatshirt in for a worn T-shirt that said, Teachers Do It With CLASS! Madison lay at her feet, slowly twitching her tail in sedate contentment.

His traitor dog opened one eye and glanced at him dismissively before deciding—with a sigh—to ignore him.

Mattie looked sorely tempted to follow her namesake's example. She shuffled the cards twice more, and he could sense that she was watching him from her peripheral vision. Mattie had never been able to hold a grudge and he could see her annoyance beginning to crumble.

Finally she held out the cards to him and asked, "You wanna play?"

Oh, boy, did he ever.

The way his pulse leaped at her suggestive invitation, he definitely wanted to play. But not cards. Not even poker. Something with higher stakes.

Then he thought of how hesitant she'd been to let him stay, how hesitant she seemed to even share his company. By offering to play cards, she seemed to be extending an olive branch. He was tempted to play, but considering how his competitiveness had annoyed Ginger, he thought better of it. He didn't want to piss her off.

He lowered himself to the chair beside her. Her T-shirt hid her generous curves. Which was probably just as well. She was enough of a distraction as it was.

Still holding the deck of cards, she said, "Five-card stud. Nothing wild. Isn't that the way you like it?"

Actually, he'd like it very wild. Wild, hot and out of control. Then he remembered she was asking about cards, not sex.

He shook his head, both in answer to her question and to clear it. "I don't play anymore."

Her curiosity got the better of her. "You don't play poker anymore? I find that hard to believe."

As kids, the three of them had spent hours out by the pool playing poker. He smiled at her disbelief. "Ginger didn't like it."

"She didn't like poker? No wonder you divorced her." Mattie's smile faded. "Sorry, that was tacky of me."

It wasn't just poker Ginger hadn't liked. She'd criticized anything competitive he did. *You never know when to let it go,* she'd said. *Over and over.*

He didn't bother to correct Mattie.

When he said nothing, she swung her legs over the side of her lounge chair and sat up to face him. Bracing her elbows on her knees, she shuffled the cards. As the cards arched against her palms and fluttered into a stack, she said, "Can I assume she didn't like card tricks, either?" She didn't wait for him to answer but fanned out the cards, facedown. "Take one."

He pulled out a card and glanced at it. King of hearts. He slid the card back into her deck without comment.

She bit down on her lip, concentrating as if trying to remember exactly how the trick worked. Finally she looked back up at him, her brow furrowing in thought, her green eyes serious.

She smiled and, closing the gap between them, she reached into his front shirt pocket and pulled out a card.

She glanced at it, then handed it back to him. "King of hearts. Interesting choice. Though—under the circumstances—perhaps not entirely appropriate."

"Did I teach you that trick?"

She settled back onto the chaise and shuffled the cards again. "Nope. You wouldn't teach me any of your tricks."

"What would have been the point? I learned most of them just to stump you."

Her mouth parted in surprise. Then she blushed. Ducking her head, she asked, "You sure you don't want to play?"

This time, she sounded as if she genuinely wanted to

play with him. Which made saying no even harder. But if—as Ginger had said—competition made him arrogant and annoying, did he really want to risk pissing her off? "I'm sure."

"Afraid you'll lose?"

"I never lose."

Instead of being annoyed by that comment, Mattie grinned. "All this and modest, too? You haven't changed a bit."

"You have, though."

She blinked, surprise written clearly in her expression. "Really? How?"

"You never used to be this...sassy."

She laughed. "Oh, yes, I did. You're just being polite."

"I bet you still drive your father crazy."

Looking thoroughly shocked, she pressed her palm to her chest. "Me?"

"Nice try. Tell it to someone who doesn't remember what a little hellion you were."

Brad remembered well enough how Coach Wilcox would wonder out loud how one little girl could cause more problems than a whole team of football players. Always the tomboy, she'd follow her father's players around and egg them into tossing the ball with her. She'd been like the team mascot. Every guy's kid sister. Until the day he noticed her tomboy clothes hid a very feminine body and he realized she wasn't such a kid anymore.

He forced his thoughts back to the present. "How's

your father doing?" he asked, because it seemed a neutral topic.

"Good," she said. "It's a shame you can't stay longer. He'd have loved to see you. But he won't be back till August."

"He's not here now?"

She shook her head. "He's been spending his summers in Mexico to work on his Spanish. With all the Mexican-American kids in the school district, he says it makes him a better teacher." She shuffled the cards again, then asked, "So what about your dad? Are you planning on seeing him while you're in town?"

"He's usually in Sacramento this time of year."

"That's not too far. You could drive down for the day."

For her it was so simple. If family was nearby, you went to see them. Relationships in his own family had never worked like that. "He and I don't talk much." Her eyes flashed with regret, and before she could offer up any consolations, he added, "I don't think he approves of what I do."

She raised her eyebrows. "You graduated from Harvard. Own your own business. And—according to Jessica—make tons of money. I find it hard to believe he's not proud of you."

"Last time we spoke he wanted to know why I wasn't parlaying all of this into a political career."

"Ouch." She winced comically. "Well, if it's any consolation, my father's proud of you. You've become a standard part of his beginning-of-the-year pep talk to the new football players."

A wave of guilt-tinged nostalgia washed over him. Why hadn't he kept in touch with Coach Wilcox? The man had been his mentor.

"Do you work at the high school with him?" he asked her.

"Huh?"

He pointed to her shirt. She looked down, clearly confused. Then she smiled. "Ah. No, I taught middle school. But I don't anymore."

"And now?"

"Now I run my grandmother's store." A hint of wistfulness laced her words.

Hoping she'd reveal more, he said, "I read that over fifty percent of teachers leave the profession within the first five years. Must be tough."

"It is. But it's great, too. Kids have so much energy. So much hope." She pulled a rubber band from her pocket and wrapped it around the playing cards. "I still miss it sometimes."

Hiding his satisfaction, he asked, "Then why'd you leave?"

"Grandma needed someone to take over."

He thought briefly of Mrs. Wilcox—with her cap of gray hair, her bustling energy, and faint perfume of cinnamon. Even before Mattie and her father moved back to live with the Wilcoxes after Mattie's mother died, Mrs. Wilcox had welcomed the neighborhood children into her home. He hadn't realized that she'd passed away and he felt an unexpected surge of loss.

Mattie paused, then cleared her throat before continuing. "She'd owned A Stitch in Time for nearly forty years. If I hadn't promised to take things over, her life's work would have been gone." She snapped her fingers. "Just like that."

"What about *your* life's work? You must have resented giving up a job you loved."

She cocked her head to the side, seeming to consider this for a moment. Whatever regret he thought he might have seen in her expression faded. "Naw. I work with great people at a job I enjoy. I have no regrets."

Despite her reassurances, he couldn't help asking, "None?"

She shook her head, the fading light catching the highlights of her hair. The cropped cinnamon waves weren't elegant or glamorous, but they framed her face well. More importantly, they suited her. Playful yet silky, spunky yet sensual. A powerful combination, one that lent her a sexual aura that even Ginger's leggy beauty couldn't match.

"Well, I don't think anyone has no regrets," she admitted. "But for the most part, life's not that bad."

The thought of Ginger left a bitter aftertaste. "Things don't always turn out the way we plan."

"Goodness, no." She chuckled. "But sometimes that's for the best. What we plan isn't always what's good for us."

"You sound like you're speaking from experience."

"Oh, I am. At sixteen I thought I knew exactly where I'd be in ten years. At twenty-six I realized there's no point in trying to plan that far ahead."

"Where did you think you'd be?"

"You really want to know?"

Surprisingly, he did. "Absolutely."

"Oookaay." She slanted him a look full of mischief. "Well, you and I are married."

"We are?"

"Oh, yeah. At sixteen, I thought you were everything I wanted in a husband."

Her honesty surprised him. As a preteen, she'd done little to hide her crush on him. At first, he'd been flattered but uninterested. By the time she'd been old enough to stir his interest, he'd been playing ball for her father's team for three years. So when her father asked him to back off, he had.

Now he couldn't help wondering if there'd been more to her crush than he'd expected. But, unlike when she'd talked about the store, her tone held no regret. Only whimsy.

He couldn't resist playing along. "Tell me about us. What kind of couple are we?"

Her lips curved into a smile every bit as playful as the glint in her eyes. "The perfect couple of course."

"How did we fall in love?" It wasn't the only question he had about this little fantasy of hers, but it was probably the safest.

"Over Christmas, while you were still in college." She tilted her head back, her eyes drifting closed. "Our first kiss was like a scene out of a movie. Passing through a doorway, we got caught under the mistletoe. You kissed me because it was tradition, but we both felt something more." She paused, caught up in the memory of things never done. "The next week, you drove Jessica and me to a New Year's Eve party. You claimed you didn't want us out on the road with so many drunk drivers. But at midnight, you made sure you and I were alone."

Her words stirred a memory. Years ago, he had driven them to a New Year's Eve party...no, not New Year's Eve. Halloween. She'd been dressed as a tawny striped cat. Her leotard had accentuated her budding curves and the tail had drawn his attention to her petite but nicely rounded bottom. The following Christmas he'd made damn sure he wasn't around whenever she'd stopped by the house. At nineteen, the three years separating their ages seemed impenetrable.

Now, three years seemed like nothing and he cursed his "noble" instincts. "Then what happened?"

Her eyes snapped open. She blinked as if waking from a dream. She turned toward him again, just enough for him to see the blush creeping across her cheeks. "Just your basic falling in love and getting married kind of stuff."

But her blush gave her away. There was more, much more to that part of the fantasy. His body clamored to hear it. Logic, however, prevailed and he forced himself to change the subject.

"If I remember right, you always wanted to join the Peace Corps."

She shot him a surprised look. "I can't believe you remember that."

He laughed. "Where was it you wanted to go? Panama or something?"

"Brazil, actually. In the rain forest."

"The rain forest? Are you sure you didn't just want

to vacation in Brazil? Carnival in Rio is supposed to be spectacular."

She wrinkled her nose in exaggerated disgust. "Yes, I'm sure."

He shook his head. "I can't imagine living in such poverty."

But Mattie? He could easily imagine her in the Peace Corps. He pictured her as she'd been in high school, hair pulled back in a ponytail, face free of makeup, dressed in no-nonsense jeans and a T-shirt as she lugged football equipment out to the field or helped her grandfather with the yard work.

He could imagine her like that now—the perfect complement to an exotic, lush landscape—smiling, her face flushed with exertion as she playfully goaded others into enjoying the hard work.

He could also imagine living out the fantasies he'd had back in high school. Luring her away from the crowd to some secluded spot where he'd pull the T-shirt from her body and lavish attention on every inch of her sun-kissed skin.

Forget the Peace Corps. He could imagine doing that damn near anywhere.

She eyed him speculatively and he was glad she couldn't read his thoughts. She'd kick his butt right out onto the street.

And he'd probably deserve it. He hadn't come for this. He had no intention of spending these two weeks lusting after his high school crush. He hadn't planned on even seeing her. Until this afternoon, Mattie had been safely relegated to the realm of "the one that got away."

And if they were going to spend the next two weeks in the same house, she'd probably better stay there.

Trying to remind himself of that, he teased her, "So what did you want to do in the Peace Corps? Bring medical supplies to the needy? Build schools for the impoverished? Heal the sick and dying?"

She laughed. "Hey, it was my fantasy. I could make myself as saintly as I wanted to be."

With a languorous stretch, she stood, a clear cue she was done reminiscing. But Brad wasn't ready to let her go yet. Not even close.

He stood, too, angling himself between the house and her chair. Before she could shy away from him, he gave in to the urge to touch an errant lock of her hair. As he toyed with the strand, he couldn't help treading into dangerous territory. "What about the fantasies where you're not saintly. Do you want to share any of those?"

4

MATTIE BLINKED in surprise. "I didn't have many of those when I was sixteen."

The glimmer of awareness in her eyes assured him she was lying. "And now?"

She didn't flinch. "Now, those are the fantasies I don't share with anyone."

But he saw in her eyes a hesitation, as if—despite her denials—she wanted to share those fantasies with him.

He could have just asked...allowed her the chance to say more. Instead, he gave in to the impulse that had been driving him all afternoon. The impulse to pull her into his arms. To taste her mouth. To find out if she really was as sweet and as hot as he'd always imagined. To just kiss her.

Her lips were pliant and he could almost taste her surprise as they opened beneath his. Her mouth still held the lingering flavor of her last sips of beer, the hint of hops; pleasant but unexpected. Faint, but powerful. Just like the scent of her.

He felt her hand reaching up to rest on his arm, her breath quickening to match his. Her body arching toward him in a gesture of unconscious acquiescence. He pulled her closer to him, one hand at her hip, the other burrowing into her hair at the nape of her neck. Her skin was velvety and warm, so soft he wanted to taste everywhere he touched. And everywhere he hadn't yet touched.

A potent rush of excitement washed over him as he felt her reaction to him. It mingled with his desire, heating his blood, driving him to deepen the kiss. To mold her body to his, to explore not only her mouth, but all the secret, dark places of her body. To possess her until she surrendered completely.

As soon as his control began to slip he pulled back. Dropping his hands, he stepped aside to let her pass.

In the moment it took her eyes to flutter open, he had to tighten his rein on his reaction to her. Bathed in moonlight, she was so damn beautiful. So damn vulnerable.

He ached to both take her and protect her. Too bad he couldn't do one without sacrificing the other.

When her eyes finally opened, they were filled with questions. He gave her the only answer he could. "I probably shouldn't have done that."

Her eyes flashed from sensual compliance to frustrated annoyance. "Why? Because I'm like a sister to you?"

No.

Because she'd never been like a sister to him. And because he'd never again be able to lie to himself and claim she was.

With a shake of her head, she started back for the house. *"Boa noite."*

As she moved, he grabbed her wrist, her pulse leaping under his fingertips. She looked sharply from her arm to his face, her fleeting expression of intense long-ing momentarily stealing his words.

Finally, he asked, "So did you ever join the Peace Corps?"

She extracted her wrist from his grasp. "No."

"Why not?"

"I married Mike instead."

And apparently her husband, unlike the imaginary one she'd dreamed of at sixteen, hadn't been willing to give up two years of his life so she could fulfill her dream. It sounded like a dream she still harbored. *Boa noite* sounded like Portuguese, the language she would have spoken had she joined the Peace Corps. Part of her must still yearn for everything she'd given up for her husband.

Selfish bastard. Mike, whoever he was, deserved to be shot.

Brad couldn't help noticing the irony, though. Gin-ger had called him a selfish bastard more times than he could count. And now—when he was trying so hard not to be a selfish bastard—he couldn't shake the feel-ing he'd done it again.

Suddenly he felt the need to make amends, not only for his own failings, but for her ex's as well.

"Mattie, I..." She paused by the door and turned to look at him again. "I'm sorry your life didn't turn out as planned."

Her face was half-hidden in the shadows, obscuring her expression. Her lips twisted into a smile, but un-able to see her eyes, he couldn't tell if humor or bitter-sweet regret fueled it.

"I'm not," she insisted. "Remember? No regrets. Besides," she added, "like I said before, we don't always know what's good for us."

Ain't that the truth.

This time, she slipped through the door before he could stop her. For a long time after she'd gone in, he stayed by the pool watching the reflection of the ascending moon.

She was right, he realized. The young didn't know what was good for them. At twenty-four he'd married Ginger, attracted to her beauty, social poise and appetite for sex. He thought she was everything he could ever want, gracious and charming in public, passionate in private.

God, had he been wrong. He'd tried to make it work. For seven long years he'd stuck with her, burying himself in his work to make up for his unhappiness at home. But the only thing more important to him than his business was having a family.

Not like the cold, sterile family he'd grown up in, but a real family. The kind that played flag football on the front lawn at Thanksgiving. That had birthday parties with crazily decorated homemade cakes. Silly Fourth-of-July celebrations, with hot dogs burning on the grill and jumbo packages of firecrackers bought by the side of the road. And honest-to-God real apple pie, fresh from the oven.

Who was he kidding? He wanted Mattie's family. Her family had been unconventional. She'd lost her mother at a young age then she'd been raised by her father and her grandparents. But her family had still been more real to him than his had. Her family had had a warmth that his family—with all its wealth and social prestige—simply couldn't match.

When he and Ginger had dated, she'd seemed perfect. At parties and social events, she'd been the center of attention. She was always so warm and charming, and he'd believed she'd be both the perfect asset to his career and the perfect mother for his children.

But after they married, something had changed. She'd grown more and more dissatisfied with their life together. Colder and more withdrawn. When she'd finally made it clear that she had no intention of carrying a child and even less interest in raising someone's brats, he'd called it quits. He'd never been sure if she'd genuinely hated children or merely said what she'd known was guaranteed to drive him away.

Looking back on it, he was surprised he'd lasted as long as he had.

No regrets, Mattie had said. He had nothing but regrets. And now, after listening to her weave that fantasy of hers, he had even more.

Mattie as a teenager had been delightful. Fun, open and loving. But her father had told him beyond a doubt that she was too young for a serious relationship.

Mattie'd made it clear she no longer mourned the life she'd once imagined them living together. She'd fallen in love with someone else. Married and lived with another man. A man who'd hijacked her dreams and broken her heart. She must have loved her husband very much to have no regrets about the sacrifices she'd made. Maybe she still loved him.

All of which only complicated their situation more. Seeing Mattie again after all these years only stirred up the attraction he'd felt for her back in high school. He was no longer her father's quarterback and she was no longer too young. But whether she knew it or not, she was still emotionally vulnerable.

With the kind of chemistry they had, a few simple kisses would lead to hours—if not days—together in bed. But what if she wanted more?

Marriage to him had already made one warm and loving woman miserable. There was no way in hell he'd risk having Mattie look at him with the same kind of contempt Ginger had.

So as tempted as he was to follow Mattie back into the house and explore that sassy little mouth of hers, he just couldn't risk it. He had to keep his hands and desires under control. Which meant the next two weeks were going to be hell.

NO REGRETS? No regrets my ass.

The thought echoed through her mind with every heart-pounding, knee-rattling step Mattie took along the bark-strewn jogging path. Squinting against the morning sun, she caught a glimpse of the last mile marker.

Okay, you can do it. Only one more mile. One. More. Mile.

She shoved aside thoughts of the pain and concentrated on putting one foot in front of the other. But no matter how she tried, she couldn't shove aside thoughts of Brad as easily.

Every time she pushed his image away, it crept back in when she wasn't looking. Mercilessly, relentlessly. And as annoying as hell.

She'd spent most of her life dreaming of what it would be like to be kissed by Brad Sumners. At eleven, she'd imagined a chaste peck on the cheek. At fourteen, she'd longed for a romantic kiss, like something out of a movie. But last night's kiss wasn't at all what she'd bargained for. It was neither chaste nor charming. She hadn't imagined the rough rasp of his fingertips against her skin, or the moist heat of his mouth as it captured hers; or the hard pulse of desire he'd stirred within her.

She still couldn't believe he'd kissed her last night. Couldn't believe he'd stopped. Couldn't believe he'd apologized.

All her life, she'd been haunted by him. By the idea of him.

Back in college, when he'd announced his engagement to Ginger, she'd been devastated. He'd invited her to the wedding, but she hadn't gone. Oh, she'd intended to go. She'd RSVPed accordingly. She'd picked out her date and her dress. Then, four hours before they were supposed to leave, she'd feigned a case of food poisoning and called to cancel.

So, instead of watching the boy she'd yearned for most of her life marry someone else, she'd cranked up the air conditioner in her dorm room and spent the weekend huddled under her down comforter, eating hot fudge straight out of the can, watching old movies...and crying.

Three months later, when Mike Johnston asked her to marry him, she'd said yes. The only thing she'd done in her life more stupid than eating a quart of hot fudge in one sitting had been marrying Mike Johnston.

To this day, the thought of either made her sick to her stomach.

She didn't blame Brad for her own stupidity. Not exactly.

Sure, he was exhibit A in her museum of personal romantic misery. He was the forerunner of a series of bad boyfriends, not to mention one useless husband. The progenitor of all her heartache, because no one had ever been able to live up to the standard he'd set so early on in her life.

Whenever Mike had stayed out late without calling or had forgotten her birthday, she'd thought, "Brad wouldn't treat me like this." All the times Mike had belched at the dinner table or fallen asleep in front of the TV with a half-empty beer can by his side, she'd thought, "Brad would have been more of a gentleman." Worst of all, every time Mike had left her unsatisfied in bed, every time he'd rushed through the foreplay and climaxed before she'd had a chance to get there, she'd thought, "Brad would have been a better lover."

She knew it was wrong. Knew it was disloyal. Knew—in her heart—that it did as much damage to her marriage as all of Mike's inconsiderate behavior. Still, she'd been unable to rein in her imagination. Every time that familiar feeling of dissatisfaction had crept into her heart, she'd yearned for Brad to sweep back into her life and take her away from everything. Take her away to some exotic locale where they'd lie on the beach and make love under the stars.

Well, she was tired of holding her life up to a fantasy. Tired of having her life fall short. It was time she put her fantasies to rest.

Brad was going to help her do it.

He'd only be here for two weeks. That wouldn't be enough time to hear him belch at the dinner table or watch him sleep in front of the TV. Certainly not enough time for him to forget her birthday.

But it would be plenty of time for them to have some really rotten sex. Clumsy. Impatient. Uninspired. Any of it would do, as long as it was bad. As long as it proved, once and for all, that Brad was not the perfect, patient, incredibly erotic, always-in-control lover of her dreams.

The way she saw it, Brad was like a card trick. Her fantasies of him were just illusions. Sleight of hand.

Back in school, it had driven her crazy wondering how he'd done those card tricks. But once she learned how to do them herself, they couldn't hold her interest. Finally having Brad would produce the same effect.

Now all she had to do was get him into bed. Seduce the man of her fantasies? Piece of cake.

5

GIVING IN TO her body's demands, Mattie slowed her pace to a walk. A few more twists in the path and she'd be back where she'd started at the entrance to the park, just a few blocks from Jessica's house. She rounded the next bend and saw Brad heading straight toward her.

Mattie stopped. Propping her hands on the tops of her thighs, she bent over, struggling to pull air into her lungs. She blinked her eyes into focus, staring at the toes of her white Reebok cross-trainers. She tried to slow her breathing by inhaling through her nose, and the astringent aroma of the cedar mulch hit her nostrils.

Slowly she straightened, until she stood upright, propping her hands low on her back. She twisted to one side and then the other to loosen her muscles.

Jeez, this was just her luck.

At least yesterday under the towel, she'd been clean. Today she was just sweaty. And she harbored no illusions whatsoever that she merely "glowed." Unless he had some weird sweaty-female fetish, she'd have to put off her big seduction plans until this evening.

Naturally Brad looked great. From the tips of his leather loafers to the top of his Titleist baseball cap and every denim-and-cotton-covered inch in between.

As soon as Madison saw her, she began pulling frantically on the leash. In a few short seconds, the dog had guided Brad straight to her.

He smiled at Mattie, that same damn charming smile that made her insides melt into goo. "Hey, Mattie. You don't mind if we join you, do you?"

She crouched beside the dog, letting Madison sniff her fingers, then leaned forward to scratch behind her ears.

Glancing up at him, Mattie sucked in a deep breath, desperately trying to get more oxygen into her bloodstream. "No." She surprised herself by relenting to temptation. "I was going to walk this last mile anyway."

The dog leaned into Mattie's touch, her eyes rolling back and her pink tongue dangling out one side of her mouth. Madison sat, then seconds later rolled onto her side exposing her belly. Taking the dog's cue, Mattie trailed her fingernails along the soft fur of Madison's chest.

"She likes you," Brad said.

Maddie looked up, suddenly aware of their positions. She all but knelt at his feet. How fitting. Sometimes she felt as if she'd spent her life like this. Kneeling at his feet—at the altar of Saint Brad.

Still, she was proud of what she'd accomplished.

Mattie stood, even though her legs trembled with the effort. She wished she could pretend her quivering muscles were due entirely to the strain of exercise. Unfortunately, she wasn't so sure.

Madison, unwilling to be ignored, rolled to her feet

and once again nudged her head against Mattie's hand.

Luckily, before Mattie could make any more of an ass out of herself by babbling like an idiot, something dashed by and caught Madison's attention.

The dog lurched, yanking Brad forward. Caught off guard, he stumbled after Madison for a few steps before pulling her back under control.

With Madison still tugging on the leash, he turned back to Mattie. As she approached, she noticed his cheeks had reddened slightly. She barely heard him mutter, "Squirrels."

"Excuse me?"

"Maddie here still wants to chase squirrels. I can't seem to break her of the habit."

"She's new, isn't she?"

"Yeah. How'd you know?"

"When my divorce went through, I spent a full week visiting the pound every day looking at kittens. If Jessica wasn't so gestapo-ish about cat hair, I would have a whole herd." They walked along in silence for a moment, then she said, "Clearly you bought the dog so you'd have someone to play with. Why don't you play with her?"

For a moment he looked at her as if she was crazy. "Someone to play with?"

"Yeah. A playmate. When you get divorced, you're suddenly all alone. So you go out and get a pet to replace the playmate you lost."

"I'm an adult. I don't need a playmate."

"Brad, even adults need someone to play with. Besides, dogs are pack animals. They have to bond with their humans before they mind them.''

''They do?''

''Yes.'' And that's when she realized she was babbling about squirrels and packs of dogs. Quite the master of seduction, wasn't she?

Figuring it couldn't get much worse than this and now would be as good a time as any to get this out of the way, she plunged right in. ''Why do you think you need advice from a woman?''

For a long moment, Brad said nothing. A frown settled on his face, then he said, ''Before she left, Ginger told me I didn't know crap about women.''

''That's what you need advice about? Ginger insulted you and you need advice about it?'' She nearly laughed out loud. ''Okay, here's my advice—ignore her.''

''It's not that simple. She knows me better than anyone.''

''People say nasty things during a divorce. I called my ex pond scum, but that doesn't mean he's a single-celled organism that can reproduce asexually.''

''Normally, I'd agree with you—if there wasn't empirical evidence to suggest otherwise.''

She faked a cough to hide her laughter, then asked, ''Empirical evidence?''

Brad, still completely serious, nodded. ''Certain events in my life suggest she may be right. I can't make a woman happy.''

For a moment, she merely stared at him. The notion that he couldn't make a woman happy was laughable.

Just standing next to him made her all gooey with endorphins. She imagined most females between the ages of two and one hundred and two would react the same.

But she could tell from the set of his jaw he took this seriously. Telling him he looked really dreamy wouldn't vanquish his doubts.

"Okay, Brad. You have to give me more details. What's the empirical evidence?"

"Jess didn't want me to come visit."

"Jess has been swamped at work lately. It's not that she didn't want you to come. It's just that she's been busy."

"Right."

"I'm not just saying that. I live with her, remember."

"Well…"

She glanced at Brad and was surprised to see that his mouth had curved into a look of confusion.

"What else?" she prompted.

"Denise, my assistant, quit."

"So hire a new assistant."

"I don't want another assistant. Denise has worked for me for over five years. Besides, if the problem is me—if I don't know how to be a good boss—then hiring a new assistant isn't going to solve the problem."

"Tell me something. What is it exactly you do?"

"I'm a business consultant."

"And what kind of consulting do you do?"

"I work with small businesses. Mostly computer companies, but others as well. People with great ideas and skills but no business sense. I help them work more efficiently. But I can't do my job without Denise.''

"Look, I'm sure you're a fine boss.''

He arched an eyebrow, shooting her a look that clearly doubted her ability to judge his managerial skills.

"I've never even met Denise, but I can extrapolate based on what I know about you.''

"And that is?'' he asked, his doubt written clearly in his gaze.

He was kidding, right? She shot him a surreptitious glance. Jeez, she could fill an entire Hello Kitty diary with what she knew about Brad.

No wait...she'd done that when she was twelve.

Figuring it was best to skip her own empirical evidence and go straight for her deduction, she asked, "Since Ginger left you, how many hours a week have you been working?''

Brad shrugged. "I don't know. Why?''

"More than before the divorce?''

"Probably.''

"And you expected Denise to work as well, didn't you?''

He hesitated.

"I bet you did. There's your problem. If you want your assistant back, all you have to do is give her a call, promise her a fifty-hour workweek, and give her an extra week of vacation. Increasing her salary won't hurt, either. Problem solved.''

"Maybe the problem with my assistant, but not the problem in general.''

"You mean the 'you don't know how to treat women' problem?"

He nodded.

"I told you, just because Ginger is a manipulative...person, that doesn't mean you have a problem."

"Even my dog trainer quit. She said I was impossible to work for."

"That's probably for the best. Your dog doesn't need a trainer. She needs you."

"Mattie," he said in obvious exasperation. "My own mother isn't returning my calls."

She stifled her laughter, or most of it anyway. "Right about now, your mother is on Saint Barts. Or Saint Martin, I'm not sure which."

"Excuse me?"

"She and your Aunt Phyllis are on a Caribbean cruise."

"They are?"

"Yes." This time she didn't bother to hide her laughter. "You gave it to them for Christmas last year. I can't believe you've forgotten."

"I...um..."

"Let me guess. Denise does all your Christmas shopping?"

He squared his shoulders, but his expression was sheepish. "Well, yes. It's standard procedure."

"I'm sure when she gets back, she'll return your calls. In fact, she'll probably be thrilled to talk to you."

Damn, she was better at this than she'd thought. She'd pretty much solved all of Brad's problems in one day. Hopefully, getting him to solve hers would be just as easy.

And here she'd been worried about her heart. Her heart hadn't even had time to throw itself in his path.

Feeling very pleased with herself, she continued. "Clearly you need to pay a little more attention to the women in your life. You shouldn't feel bad about it. Most men make that mistake. You know, you might want to buy some self-help books. *Men Are from Mars, Women Are from Venus,* that kind of thing."

He shook his head. "If I had time for that I wouldn't need your advice."

She frowned. "If this is really important to you, you'll make the time."

He opened his mouth as if to say something, but then snapped it closed, leaving her wondering if she'd somehow misinterpreted something he'd said. They reached the end of the jogging path and Mattie turned down the block toward home. Feeling cocky, she asked, "What else you got for me?"

Brad didn't answer right away. In fact, he was silent for so long, she glanced over her shoulder to find him walking several paces behind her, shoulders stooped ever so slightly, a pensive expression on his face.

She stopped and waited for him to catch up with her. "What is it? Is there anything else you need help with?"

"Actually, you know my birthday is coming up…"

He trailed off and she sensed there was something he left unsaid. And that whatever he wasn't saying was very important.

Jessica had also mentioned his upcoming birthday. It'd be his thirty-third, if she remembered correctly. Exactly fifteen years since he'd been a senior in high school.

He stared absently down the street, his hands shoved in his pockets. "Next time around I don't want to make the same mistakes."

She couldn't help thinking about the mistakes she'd made and silently agreed. No regrets was fine, but no mistakes would be better.

And that's when everything clicked into place in her mind. Brad's upcoming birthday, his obsession with goals, and the fifteen years that had passed since high school.

Suddenly suspicious, she stopped in her tracks. "Give me your wallet."

He blinked in surprise. "What?"

"You heard me. Give me your wallet."

"What are you doing? Mugging me?"

She groaned in frustration. "Now."

He raised his eyebrows but reached into his back pocket and withdrew his wallet, handing it over to her without comment.

She flicked open the supple leather with a snap of her wrist. Ignoring the cash and a bevy of yellow receipts, she thumbed through the slots where he kept his credit cards.

She didn't see it right away, but that didn't discourage her. It had to be here. It just had to.

Mrs. Winslow, Palo Verde High's twelfth-grade English teacher, always spent the first week of school preaching about goal setting. At the end of that first week, she handed out business-card-sized goal charts where she had her students write down their goals for life in five-year increments.

Most students threw theirs out. Her own card had gone straight into a desk drawer, never to be seen again. But Brad had made a big deal about carrying his in his wallet all through his senior year. And if she knew him half as well as she thought she did...

"Aha!" She snatched the card from its hiding place behind a Platinum VISA. She frowned, then looked back up at Brad. "You had it laminated?"

His eyes narrowed and he reached for the card. She tossed him his wallet instead. She used the seconds it took him to fumble with the wallet to study the card.

Next to age eighteen, he'd written "Attend Harvard—on scholarship." He'd done that. By twenty-three, he'd written "Start own business." He'd done that. By twenty-eight, "Have net worth exceeding one million dollars." While she didn't know for sure, she'd be willing to bet her own measly net worth he'd met that goal as well.

Once again, Brad reached for the card. She dodged out of his grasp and read the words next to thirty-three.

Just as she thought.

He plucked the card from her fingertips just as she said the words aloud. "'Have family—i.e., wife and minimum one child.'"

6

"ARE YOU CRAZY?"

Brad considered her question as he slid the laminated card back in his wallet. Crazy? He didn't think so.

Confused? That was another matter entirely.

He'd achieved every major goal he'd set for himself in the past fifteen years. Now—when it mattered most—he'd failed. What he couldn't figure out was why it pissed her off.

"Look Mattie, all I—"

She cut him off with a vehement shake of her head. "No. Absolutely not."

"But—"

"I am *not* going to help you find a wife."

"Find a wife?" It took him a second to comprehend the conclusion she'd leaped to. By that time, she'd already spun on her heel and stormed off down the street.

He caught up with her in a few steps, but she refused to look over at him. "I don't need—"

She jerked to a stop, then whirled around. "*You* don't need? This is all about what you need, isn't it?" She glared at him, her eyes shooting daggers. "What about what I need?"

It was just as well she didn't give him a chance to answer. He didn't have the slightest idea how to respond.

"I'll tell you what I don't need. I don't need this. I don't need you here complicating my life. I've got problems of my own, you know. I've got employees who depend on me. I've got taxes to pay. I've got a business that's about to go under. And that's just work.

"I've got a whole host of personal problems as well. So if it's okay with you, I'll just let you find your own wife. I'm sure you'll be as super successful as always once you put your mind to it."

Before he even had a chance to respond, she turned and stomped off. This time, he didn't follow her.

He valued his hide. And right now, sweet little Mattie Wilcox looked mad enough to strip that hide right off him.

Maybe he'd wait until she calmed down before telling her how completely she'd misread the situation.

"GIVE ME ADVICE, Mattie," Mattie mimicked in a high childish voice as she slammed the butcher knife into the carrot, chopping the vegetable with a forceful whack.

Thirteen hours had passed since she'd run into Brad at the park. Unfortunately, those hours had done little to lessen her anger. The time she'd spent doing inventory in the empty space above her store hadn't helped, either. The work had left her with too much time for her anger to simmer.

"Tell me how to treat women, Mattie." *Whack.*

"Help me find a wife, Mattie." *Whack, whack, whack.*

She surveyed the remaining ingredients before purposefully selecting another carrot. "You're just like a sister to me, Mattie."

Whack, whack, whack, whack.

She paused, knife raised, and assessed the damage she'd done. Uneven chunks of carrot lay scattered across the cutting board.

Why was she so angry?

So he wanted to get married again? What was so wrong with that?

"Because," she defended to herself, "a wife isn't just something you order out of a catalog. That isn't the way it works."

So all of this righteous indignation was on behalf of his future wife? Some woman she'd never met, some woman he hadn't even decided on.

Or is it the final reminder that—after all these years— Brad still doesn't have the slightest idea you're a woman. He still sees you as a kid sister. Androgynous. Sexless. Safe.

All of which put a serious kink in her plans. If he truly saw her as a kid sister—as Jessica had claimed he still did—she'd never get him into bed. Even if his kiss had turned her to jelly, it obviously had had no effect on him.

At this rate, she'd never get over Brad Sumners.

She sighed, blowing her bangs out of her eyes, then reached for the grater and started grating the carrot chunks for the zucchini muffins.

Taking out her anger on the carrots was hardly the adult thing to do—especially given their shape and resemblance to a certain portion of male anatomy—but it did give her a perverse sense of satisfaction.

She scraped the carrots into a waiting bowl then reached for a zucchini. As she julienned the zucchini, she felt a steely edge of determination harden within her.

He thought of her as a kid sister? Well, guess what, she wasn't his kid sister. He didn't see her as a woman? Too bad. She'd just have to make him. No more Ms. Nice Sprout. Brad Sumners was about to meet the real Mattie Wilcox.

ON THE OTHER SIDE of the house, Mattie heard a door open and close. She paused, listening intently. When she'd returned from the shop, the house had been silent. She'd assumed he was asleep. Apparently she was wrong.

Exhaling slowly, she hoped she now seemed a little less hysterical.

"You're back," Brad said, entering the kitchen.

With a sigh, Mattie set aside the cutting board and dried her hands before turning to face him. He stood just opposite her, leaning against the counter, long legs stretched out before him. Mimicking his stance, she propped her hip against the counter and crossed her arms over her chest.

Since this morning in the park, he'd lost the ball cap, but he still wore his jeans—faded denim, worn to near-white along his thighs and at the seams. He'd rolled up the sleeves of his oxford shirt to reveal his tanned forearms and his hair was tousled, as if he'd been running his fingers through it.

When her gaze finally met his, her breath caught in her throat, and she shivered at the intensity in his eyes. It was a bit disconcerting to realize he'd been studying her with the same attention to detail she'd given him, and she was uncomfortably aware that her baggy denim shorts and old T-shirt did less for her assets than his clothing did for him.

He reached into the front pocket of his shirt and withdrew a white card, which she instantly recognized as the goal card. He held it up, clasped between his forefinger and his middle finger.

"This morning, you got the wrong idea about this card." With a flick of his wrist, he tossed it onto the counter beside her.

She picked up the card automatically and studied it for a moment. "So you don't want my help finding another wife?"

"I don't want another wife."

"But you do want to be married." She flipped the card over, presenting him with his own neat handwriting. "Says so right here."

His gaze flickered to the paper and then back to her face. "I filled out that card a long time ago. I was young and stupid. I'd forgotten I still carried it."

"But at one time," she pointed out, "it meant enough to you that you had it laminated."

"Trust me. I don't want another wife. One was enough."

"If you don't want another wife, what do you want?"

He didn't answer right away and the silence seemed to stretch between them, the air in the kitchen suddenly electric.

Only then did she notice the near-empty tumbler in his other hand. A lone ice cube sat in the bottom of the glass. She glanced behind him and noticed an open bottle of Scotch on the table. Jessica kept it on hand only for when her father visited. Unless the man had been visiting a lot more than Mattie knew about, Brad had spent the evening putting a serious dent in the Scotch.

Inexplicably nervous, Mattie changed the subject, pointing at the glass with her empty hand. "You've been drinking."

"Of course I have. Under the circumstances, I thought it appropriate." He raised the glass to his lips then blinked in surprise when he realized it was empty. Before she could stop him, he poured himself another drink.

She reached for his glass just as he was raising it to his lips. "Maybe you've had enough?"

"Enough for what? Enough to admit I don't think of you as a sister?"

A shiver started in her belly and worked its way through her body all the way to her fingertips. Suddenly her blood felt as thick as her own muffin batter—too thick for her heart to pump it through her veins. She averted her eyes, wondering if the fumes from the Scotch had done something to her head.

He asked, "Didn't you ever wonder why I never asked you out?"

Surprise ricocheted through her and all she could muster in response was "Huh?" followed by a long pause and then an equally ineloquent "Well, no."

Sure, she'd fantasized endlessly about him asking her out, but she'd never wondered why he hadn't. "I was the scrawny best friend of your kid sister. I figured I was too young and you simply weren't interested."

"When you first moved to Palo Verde, when you were ten? Yeah, you were much too young."

He put his glass down and pushed away from the counter to step nearer to her.

"When you were thirteen? Yeah, you were just the scrawny best friend of my kid sister."

With two more steps, he closed the distance between them. He stopped, with his feet planted on either side of her own. Mattie's heart began to pound at his closeness. She inhaled sharply, trying to catch her breath, but that just pulled Brad's warm, masculine scent into her lungs and did nothing to clear her head.

"By the time you were fifteen? You weren't scrawny." His focus drifted from her face, down her front, lingering over her breasts. "You were still too young, but that wouldn't have made much difference."

She tried to concentrate on his words, but his nearness muddled her thoughts. Then he reached out and tucked a strand of her hair behind her ear. Even more surprising, he didn't release her hair. He clasped the lock, slowly twirling it around his forefinger so that the ends of her hair and his knuckles alternately brushed against her cheek. Mattie shivered uncontrollably.

She found herself arching up toward him, waiting for him to lower his mouth to hers, to pull her against his body. To ease the ache that had been building inside of her for years.

But he kept his distance. Just like always.

Damn it. Damn him. Damn him for being so desirable. Damn him for making her want him. For stringing her along.

Finally, she found her voice. "What are you saying, Brad?"

He leaned into her, brushing his lips against her cheek as he moved to whisper in her ear. "Remember when we used to play flag football?"

The abrupt change in topic made her head spin.

Right, that was it. The topic change, not the feel of Brad's lips against her cheek. Not the heat of his body so close to hers. Right.

Planting her hands against his chest, she tried to push him away from her. However, instead of being sent staggering backward by the momentum the way she imagined, he merely straightened. He pressed his hands onto hers, trapping her palms against his chest.

She felt his pecs tense beneath her palms. They weren't the wiry muscles of a teenage boy, but the lean, powerful muscles of a man.

A man. Not the boy she'd known, but a fully grown man. More powerful than the boy. More dangerous, too.

"You do remember flag football, don't you? We'd

play in your front yard on Saturdays. Your grandmother would serve cookies and fresh apple cider on the porch."

Despite herself, she nodded. Jessica would sit up on the porch in one of the lounge chairs, looking like a movie star as she flipped through the latest copy of *Seventeen* with her sunglasses perched on her nose and her legs stretched out in front of her. Mattie—on the other hand—would be out in the yard. Just one of the guys. Desperate for Brad's attention, even if she had to tackle him to get it.

"You never picked me to be on your team," she blurted out, not meaning it to sound like the accusation it clearly was.

"No, I didn't."

"Because I was a girl?"

"No. Because I liked to chase you."

She blinked, surprised by his answer and by the seriousness in his voice. By the pounding of his heart beneath her palm.

Jerking her hands out from under his, she sidled away from him. As she backed away, she wrapped her arms around her waist. "Stop teasing me."

Turning, he propped his hip against the counter. "You think I'm lying?"

"I think you want something and you're trying to manipulate me into giving it to you."

"What is it you think I want?"

"I don't know. But I don't for one minute believe you've spent all this time pining away for me. You probably only brought up flag football because you don't have any memories of me that aren't related to my father being the football coach.''

''Thanksgiving Day,'' he said quickly. ''You were fifteen, I was eighteen. You were dressed in jeans and a purple T-shirt. You'd borrowed my baseball cap and you wore your hair in a ponytail hanging out the back. It was the sexiest thing I'd ever seen. I spent the whole damn day chasing after you.''

Her breath came in short bursts as she remembered the day he described, the exhilaration of being chased by him, of dashing across the lawn, just out of his reach. And finally, of the firm tug as he latched onto her flag. But her flag didn't pull loose and they tumbled to the ground.

For a long moment, they'd lain there. She underneath him, his palms braced on either side of her head, holding his weight off her. Their breath mingled in the crisp November air.

''You tackled me.'' She'd waited—breathless—sure he was going to kiss her. Her first kiss from him. From anybody.

''I did.'' He nodded, looking at her from under his lashes.

But he hadn't kissed her. He'd simply stared at her, his blue eyes suddenly dark, his body lean and hot over hers, until the shrill blast from her father's whistle had punctured the moment.

''Dad penalized you for tackling me. It cost you the game.''

''It was worth it.''

"You didn't think so at the time. You were angry with him for weeks afterward."

"That's not why I was angry. I didn't give a damn about the game."

"I don't believe you. You always care about the game. Winning is everything. Isn't that what you always said?"

His lips quirked into an ironic smile. "It wasn't the game I was worried about winning."

"I don't understand."

"After the game, your father pulled me aside. He asked me to stay away from you."

It took a moment for his words to sink in. Then she blinked in surprise. "What? What do you mean, stay away from me?"

"Your father knew I was interested in you. He'd have been blind not to see it. He also knew I was too old for you. So he asked me to keep my distance until you were older."

Reeling, she took a step backward, bumping into the refrigerator. "You were interested in me?" she repeated numbly.

He nodded, moving closer. "Absolutely."

She wanted to keep him at a distance, but she had no avenue of retreat. So she braced her palms against the cool white enamel, anchoring herself to it. "But you stayed away from me, because my father asked you to."

"Yes."

As Brad closed the space between them, Mattie saw

the glimmer of regret in his eyes. Her heart sank with the realization of what her father had done.

Brad was everything she'd ever wanted. Every dream, every fantasy she'd ever had. If her father hadn't interfered, he could have been hers.

Her hands clenched into fists and she fought the urge to pound them against the refrigerator. "He had no right to—"

"He's your father. He had every right." Cupping her chin in his hand, he nudged her gaze up to his. "He did what he thought was best."

She shook her head, both in anger and denial. When she got her hands on that meddlesome old fool...

"Mattie, look at me."

She jerked her attention back to him. The sensual promise she'd seen lingering his eyes was now diluted with something else. Something more serious.

Conviction, she realized. Absolute conviction. He believed her father had done the right thing.

"Do you know what would have happened if we'd gotten involved back then?"

I would have lived out every fantasy I'd ever had. I'd have been Brad Sumner's girlfriend. I'd have known what it was like to be kissed by him. Held by him. Maybe even loved by him.

Instead of saying any of that aloud, she shook her head mutely.

"A couple of dates, a few kisses...that wouldn't have been enough. Not for me. I was eighteen, I would have wanted more than chaste kisses. Your father knew that."

"But—"

"Oh, I would have tried to be a gentleman about it. I would have tried to keep my hands off you. You were so damn young." He brushed his thumb across her cheek, down to the corner of her mouth. "So damn beautiful. And so damn eager to please me."

At his touch, her mouth dropped open and her breath came out as a sigh. She felt herself straining toward him again. Praying—nearly begging—for him to kiss her.

His gaze darkened and dropped to her lips. "I definitely would have wanted more. And you would have given it to me." Shaking his head, he dropped his hand to his side and stepped away from her. As he shoved his hand into his pocket, he said, "It pissed me off, but I knew your father was right. You were too young."

"I wouldn't have been too young forever. You couldn't have waited a year or two?" If he had, things might have turned out so differently.

For an instant, sadness flickered through his eyes. "You weren't on the card, Mattie." Then, shaking his head, he reached behind her and picked up the card she'd tossed aside earlier. "It was Harvard, business, millions, then wife and kids."

"And you don't think I would have waited?"

His answer hardly mattered, because she *wouldn't* have waited. She would have been too impatient to wait.

"It wouldn't have worked even if you had. You're a small-town girl, Mattie. You love living in a place like this. You always have. I knew I'd never come back here to live. It just wasn't meant to be. So I stayed away."

Oh, no. He wasn't going to back off again. Not after everything he'd revealed. Neither of them was a teenager anymore. It was time to put her plan of seduction into action.

Pushing away from the refrigerator, she moved toward him. "What about now, Brad? What's your excuse for staying away now?"

7

CLEARLY SHE'D CAUGHT HIM off guard.

Brad blinked in surprise, then said, "I told you before. I don't want another wife."

"Who said I want another husband?"

"You did. Last night by the pool. Whether you realize it or not, you still harbor some fantasy about us ending up together." He stopped backing away from her and before she knew it, she was standing close enough to touch him.

"Those were the fantasies I had as a teenager. Don't you want to know about the fantasies I have now? The ones where I'm not so saintly? The ones you asked about last night?"

She brought her hand to his cheek. The jutting bone of his jaw rested squarely in her palm and a day's worth of beard stubble brushed her skin. The only thing more erotic than these blatant reminders of his masculinity was the heady knowledge of her power over him.

All those years ago, she hadn't been the only one harboring secret fantasies. Tonight, she wouldn't be the only one finally acting them out.

"Mattie, this isn't a good idea."

"I think this is the best idea either of us has ever had."

Standing on tiptoe, she pressed her mouth to his. For an instant, he held himself back, his arms loose at his sides while his chest muscles tensed beneath her left palm, his jaw tightening beneath her right. She could sense his struggle with his own stringent morals—those same morals that had kept him from her all those years ago. This time, he lost.

In a flash, he went from passive to passionate. He wrapped his arms around her, lifting her from her toes as he pulled her to him. Her breath was knocked out of her from the strength of his embrace. From the strength of his response.

Cradling her against his body, he backed her up against the countertop behind her. Only when he set her down on its surface was she able to draw air into her lungs. But even then she couldn't catch her breath.

The feel of his mouth over hers was too intoxicating. As intoxicating as the expensive Scotch he tasted like. The feel of his hands on her body was too heady. They seemed to be everywhere at once. On her skin and in her hair. Tugging at her shirt and cupping her buttocks through her shorts.

She thought briefly of her stupid, stupid plan to have bad sex with him. Impatient, clumsy sex.

His impatience thrilled her and she reveled in his clumsy, grasping hands. They spoke of his passion. Of the urgency of the moment. The need to possess and claim.

A need she understood only too well as she wrapped

her legs around his waist, pulling his body closer and rocking her hips against his. The legs of her shorts sagged, leaving most of her legs bare and she savored the feel of denim against the sensitive skin of her inner thighs. She locked her ankles together behind his back, digging her heels into his buttocks.

He tore his mouth from hers to burrow at her neck. She arched up to him, baring her throat to his touch. His teeth nipped at her throat as if he would devour her.

She pressed herself against him, relishing the feel of his erection against her most sensitive flesh. Pleasure pulsed through her until she was gasping, clutching at his shoulders, nearly coming apart.

His hands gripped her thighs, pulling her closer to him as they slid up the legs of her shorts. She wished she were naked, but her baggy shorts were the next best thing. She felt his fingertips graze against her panties and she bucked her hips up, automatically giving him access.

She moaned as he slipped his thumb beneath the elastic edging. His thumb sought and found the very center of her. He stroked her, relentlessly pushing her closer to the edge. Clutching at his shoulders, calling out his name, she didn't hesitate to tumble over.

She sat, trembling in his arms, unaware of anything other than the heat of his hands on her skin, the strength of his embrace and the aching need that still pulsed through her body. Though she'd found one form of release, she wanted more. More of him, more of his body, more of his touch.

She wanted him naked and exposed to her touch. Completely at her mercy. She wanted him trembling with need, as she was. Most of all, she wanted him inside of her. Hard, thrusting and completely out of control.

Her hands tightened convulsively as she reached for the waistband on his jeans. But before she could unfasten the top button, he grabbed both of her hands in one of his.

He pressed his forehead to hers, squeezed his eyes closed. She heard him suck in a deep breath, sensed him fighting for control.

"Don't get me wrong, Sprout. You're tempting. You certainly are." Abruptly he dropped his hand and stepped away. "But I didn't want to break your heart when I was eighteen any more than I want to break it now."

Then—before she could even protest—he turned and walked away.

For a long moment, she sat on the counter, trembling, weak, and fighting to make sense of her careening emotions. She stared first at the empty doorway through which he'd just disappeared, then at the near-empty Scotch bottle.

He was walking away from her? From them?

She tugged the hem of her shirt back into place, then hopped down from the counter before straightening her shorts as well. Her knees felt weak and shaky, but she forced herself to stand.

Had she really thought sex with him would be bad?

Had she really thought this would help her get over him?

Well, it hadn't. She'd just had one of the most explosive orgasms of her life and as far as she could tell, he hadn't even been affected. He'd stayed completely in control the whole time.

And he'd been drunk.

What was he? Made of steel? Comic-book superheroes had less willpower.

And—while she was at it, damn it—how many times did she have to watch him walk away from her?

Just this morning—hell, just a few minutes ago, it seemed—she'd clung to the idea that she'd be able to banish her fantasies of Brad by acting them out. Boy, had he proved her wrong.

What would she do if sex with him lived up to or exceeded her expectations? Or worse, what would she do if she couldn't get him into bed at all?

Just live with the shadow of her dreams looming over her? That was unthinkable.

If she didn't get him into bed while he was here, she'd regret it for the rest of her life. And she was going to have to act fast. Because if she knew Brad half as well as she thought she did, when he woke up in the morning, those damn morals of his would rear their ugly heads.

He'd start feeling guilty, worrying that he had somehow taken advantage of her. And that was just the excuse he needed to walk right out of her life. Again.

But she was not going to let him do it. Not this time. She needed to find a way to keep him in Palo Verde long enough to seduce him. And if she had to, she'd use his morals and his guilt against him.

She was going to get Brad into bed and she'd use any means necessary to do it.

FIFTY POUNDS OF PRESSURE bore down on Brad's chest as he struggled into consciousness. His head pounded. His body ached. His tongue clung to the roof of his mouth—a mouth so dry it felt like someone had poured a bag of cat litter into it. To make matters worse, he had the distinct feeling that putting a good dent in Jessica's bottle of Scotch wasn't the only stupid thing he'd done last night.

Why the hell had he thought it would be a good idea to come clean with Mattie? Why the hell had he thought she needed to know how he'd felt about her back in high school? And why the hell had he given in to the need to kiss her?

As if that would ever be enough. As if he'd ever be able to kiss her again without wanting to touch her. Without wanting to strip her clothes from that luscious body. Without needing to see—once and for all—the body that had fueled his teenage fantasies. Needing to explore every responsive inch of that body. Needing to drive her completely over the edge again and again.

Needing her so badly, but still walking away from her had been one of the hardest things he'd ever done.

The acidity in his stomach churned, threatening to creep up his esophagus and douse the cat-litter grit. He swallowed hard, choking back the reflex to vomit.

Dear God, what had he been thinking?

The weight on his chest—guilt?—shifted a bit.

By force of will alone, he pried open one of his eyes. Through a hazy film, he focused on the honey-colored blob that dominated his field of vision. The blob turned and a warm gust blew across his face. A somewhat rank, warm gust.

He forced open his other eye and the blob shifted into focus. Not guilt. His dog.

A vague recollection of choosing a new name for the dog flitted through his mind but didn't stay with him. Yet every moment of his conversation with Mattie played across his mental TV screen with the startling detail of high-definition DVD. Every word. Every touch. Every tempting, begging glance.

Fighting a sense of doom, he nudged the dog off his chest and struggled into a sitting position. Blood pounded through his brain and waves of nausea rolled through his stomach. He paused, perched on the edge of the bed, hand raised to shield his eyes against a single ray of light piercing the blinds. He drew in a deep breath. Too bad he was still alive.

At least it was a weekday morning. Mattie would already be at work. Thank God he wouldn't have to face her for at least another eight hours.

The dog hopped to the floor and lunged for the closed door. He glared at her. "Don't think this means you get to sleep on the bed every night."

She scratched at the door in response and shot a pleading glance in his direction. He winced at the nerve-fraying sound of nails on wood.

"Right. We'll negotiate later." Using his arms for

support, he levered himself off the edge of the bed. As soon as he had his feet under him, the dull throb of his headache cranked up several notches. He stumbled down the hall toward the back door with his dog bounding ahead of him.

He fiddled with the latch and the dog darted out.

Only when he turned around did he see Mattie. He thanked God he'd slept in his jeans, because he hadn't even thought about putting clothes on before leaving his room. With memories of last night still flooding his system, his body wasn't really in any shape to be seen. The sight of her didn't help matters.

She sat in one of Jessica's oversize armchairs, one leg tucked under her, the other dangling over the arm. Dressed in black shorts that left the length of her tanned legs bare and a white T-shirt that clung to her breasts, she seemed completely relaxed. As unaware of her effect on him as she had been at fifteen.

Spread across her lap was a patchwork quilt of dark velvety fabrics. She held a needle in one hand and a triangle of green velvet in the other.

"You're up," she said. Then she returned her attention to the fabric in her lap. With fluid movements, Mattie sewed a delicate line of stitches.

She spread the fabric across her raised knee and ran her fingers against the nap of the velvet. The obvious sensual pleasure she took in stroking the material tugged at his imagination. The image flashed through his mind of her delicate little hands stroking his skin, roaming over her flesh and his body with that same studied thought. If he hadn't stopped last night, her hands could be touching him right now. His gut clenched, spilling heat through his body.

He cursed himself, banking the image. Keeping his hands off Mattie required every last scrap of control as it was.

Shoving his hands into the pockets of his jeans to keep himself from reaching for her, he rested his shoulder against the arched threshold of the dining room. "I didn't think you'd still be here," he admitted. Fumbling for something more to say, he pointed to the fabric on her lap. "Is that a quilt?"

She looked up. "Yes. It's called a crazy quilt. I can't force myself to make any of the standard patterns. All those squares and triangles make me cross-eyed."

"But you still make them?"

She laughed. "I still try. After all, it's what A Stitch In Time specializes in." She held up the fabric and he realized that, although she'd sewn several pieces together, she'd done it badly and the pieces didn't hang straight. "Too bad I suck, huh?"

And that was Mattie in a nutshell. She'd given up a job she loved to take over someone else's dream. Even though she didn't like to quilt, she was still taking a stab at it. She was so used to putting other people's needs before her own. If she knew how badly he wanted to stay—at least until his birthday—she wouldn't let him leave, even though it'd be easier on her if he did.

Pushing away from the doorjamb, he said, "I'm sorry if what happened last night made you uncomfortable. By the time you get home from work, Maddie and I will be gone."

There. He'd done it. Sacrificed his wants for hers.

While he didn't exactly expect her to throw herself against the door and block his exit, he was more than a little disappointed when she merely looked up at him, and said, "You mean you and Avenue will be gone."

"Excuse me?"

"Avenue." She stood, then carefully folded the patchwork of velvet down to a manageable size and dropped it into a tote bag. "Last night—after your very disappointing display of control—you decided to rename your dog." She made her way to the kitchen and grabbed an apple from the bowl on the counter. "Get it? Madison Avenue. Avenue. It's kind of cute, actually."

He couldn't seem to take his eyes off her. Never before had a woman held his attention so completely. "Okay. Avenue and I won't be here when you get home tonight."

She shook her head slowly, as if he were being particularly dense. "Oh, but you will."

"No, I—" He broke off, then studied her cheerful demeanor. Her expression indicated she knew something he didn't. "I will?"

"Yep." She sauntered back to where he stood in the doorway.

He had to force himself not to step back when she stopped mere inches away from him. But not moving away from her was ten times easier than not touching her. "Why is that?"

"You are going to stay, because you, Brad, are a nice guy." With that, she took a bite of her apple.

He should have known better than to try to have a conversation with his head still throbbing. "A nice guy?"

"Yep." She offered the apple to him as she chewed. He watched in fascination as the muscles of her neck contracted when she swallowed. "You want a bite?"

Just last night, they'd stood here in this kitchen and he'd poured his guts out to her. He'd stupidly thought getting his attraction to her out in the open would clear the air. Man, had he ever been wrong. Telling her how he'd felt made him want her more. Feeling the heat of her response only made this harder. Only made him harder.

And she seemed completely unaffected. Probably because she thought he was such a nice guy.

Before logic could prevail, he grabbed her wrist. When her eyes met his, he said, "Stop trying to tempt me, Mattie. And don't make the mistake of thinking I'm a nice guy."

8

SHE FLASHED HIM a smile full of audacity. "Oh, Brad, but you are a nice guy. Last night only proves it." She took another bite of apple. "You see, nice guys always do the right thing."

"They do?"

"Oh, yes." There was something unconsciously erotic about the sight of her white teeth sinking into the mottled red skin, about the crunch and the crisp, fresh scent.

"Back in high school," she continued, "you stayed away from me because it was the right thing to do. And last night, you didn't take me to bed because you thought it was the right thing to do. Undoubtedly out of some misguided notion that you were protecting me."

"I—" he tried to protest, but she cut him off.

"The point is, again you did the right thing. Because that's what nice guys do. And that's exactly why you will not be leaving today."

"It is?"

"Yep."

He was sure she hadn't moved, yet she seemed closer—more tempting—than she had been even a few minutes ago.

"You see, Brad, I need your help. Or rather, my shop needs your help. You said yesterday that your business is fixing businesses. Well, my business needs fixing. So, instead of leaving today, you'll stay and do what you can to help my business, because—"

"It's the right thing to do. I get it."

She smiled brightly. "Excellent. Then it's settled."

She took one last bite of apple. Then she spun around and strolled back into the kitchen. Over her shoulder, she said, "You'll help my shop, and in return, I'll help you figure out what went wrong with your marriage."

"Yesterday you—"

"Yes, I know. Yesterday I said it was all Ginger's fault. But—to be honest—I'm probably not very objective where she's concerned. It's probably a bit more complicated than that, don't you think? You said it yourself—you don't want to make the same mistakes twice. So next time around—"

"I told you I don't want—"

"I know, I know, you don't want to get married again." She waved aside his protests. "I understand you think you don't want to get married again. But your divorce has been final for what—five minutes? Everybody thinks they never want to get married again when they've just gotten divorced. Give it some time."

"Time isn't what I need."

She paused and, for the first time that morning, her playful facade fell away. After studying him for a moment, she nodded. "Time will help. Trust me. Once being married was very important to you. No matter how cynical you're feeling about Ginger right now, it's still important to you. If it wasn't, you wouldn't have come home to get advice from Jessica."

Feeling steamrollered by her energy and her scattered logic—not to mention her mere proximity—he could hardly muster an argument.

"What makes you so sure I can help your business?"

"Because." She smiled gamely. "You're Brad Sumners."

As if that explained everything.

When he stared blankly at her, she added, "You're perfect. You can do anything you put your mind to. And you always win."

I AM IN WAY OVER MY HEAD.

The words echoed through her mind as she navigated her Geo Prism through the streets of Palo Verde. Like most small towns, what little traffic there was in Palo Verde was confined to Main Street, which snaked through the center of town parallel to the river and the old train tracks. Nestled against the foothills of the Sierra Nevada Mountains, Palo Verde was just far enough east of Sacramento that few people commuted from one to the other, though she had during her marriage to Mike, since he'd wanted to live in Sacramento and she'd taken a job at the middle school here in town.

Palo Verde was the kind of town where people lived their whole lives—small, but not confined, close to the attractions of both Sacramento and Lake Tahoe. Even now, most people who grew up there settled down there, as well. She loved this town where she'd spent all of the best years of her life. And every day her heart filled with pride when she turned onto Main Street and caught sight of the two-story painted brick building that housed A Stitch in Time.

Like many of the buildings lining Main Street, A Stitch in Time was worn but charming. Its turn-of-the-century brick facade needed another coat of paint. The red-and-white For Rent sign she'd hung in the upstairs window had faded and she'd long since given up hopes of easing the store's financial burdens by renting out the office space above.

But even with all her financial problems, she wouldn't trade the shop for the world. It was a piece of her past—a piece of her. And even today, as edgy and anxious as she was, something about the sheer normalcy of pulling into the parking lot behind the store calmed her.

But not for long. Mattie clutched a stack of library books to her chest and slammed her car door shut with her foot.

"Stop being such a weenie," she ordered herself as she skulked through the back parking lot, praying she wouldn't run into anyone she knew.

Bringing her "research" books to work was a horrible risk. But a calculated one. Sure, she'd talked Brad into staying, at least for a couple of days, but she still needed a strategy for getting him into bed. Last night she'd been practically begging for it. And he'd calmly turned his back on her and just walked away. And that was with his will already weakened by alcohol.

He was going to be one tough nut to crack, in terms of a seduction. She needed to do far more than simply pique his interest. She needed to do more than merely turn him on. She needed to make him lose control completely. No small task, given his compulsive need to win all the time.

There was quite a big difference between sleeping with one's husband and seducing the man of one's sexual fantasies. She just wanted to be prepared.

Which meant she needed time to study, yet she didn't dare bring any of these books home with her. If Brad saw her reading one of them...well, he'd guess what she was up to. She'd have a hell of a time seducing him as he ran out the door.

"You can do this. You're not in over your head. You're a strong, inde—"

"Talking to yourself again?"

Her head jerked toward the unexpected voice. With her attention divided, her foot came into contact with the curb, and her legs twisted out from under her. Books flew from her grasp as she instinctively thrust her arms out to catch herself.

She landed facedown on a pile of books, her head mere inches from her store's back door.

"Omigod, omigod, omigod!" Lucy, the store's newest employee, a nineteen-year-old unwed mother-to-be, gasped the apology. "Miss Mattie, I'm so sorry!"

She lay there, pain searing her palms, trying to catch her breath. It took a second for her lungs to suck in oxygen. Slowly she turned her head only to see Lucy trying to squat by her side.

"No, stay where you are. If you kneel, we may never get you back up again. And you don't have to call me Miss Mattie, remember? I'm not your teacher anymore." Mattie shook her hands, trying to dispel the stinging, then braced herself on her palms and tried to lever herself up. She twisted into a sitting position, bumped some of the books aside with her hip, then lowered herself back to the walkway. "Jeez, for a woman eight months pregnant, you sure know how to sneak up on someone."

"Oh, gawd, I'm so sorry. I thought you knew I was there."

Lucy was dressed in bright purple corduroy overalls with a matching purple-striped shirt underneath. With her long blond hair braided into plaits on either side of her face, she looked like an enormous toddler dressed in Garanimals. Or Barney. How had she missed a Barney look-alike walking up beside her?

Mattie flicked a chunk of gravel off her palm. "Don't worry abo—"

Before she could finish the sentence, something slammed against her back. "Ow!"

"Stop!" Lucy yelled, stepping over Mattie's outstretched legs.

Mattie turned to see Lucy grabbing the door just in time to keep the damn thing from hitting her again.

Cursing her bad luck, she scooched out of the way so the door could swing open. Through the door came Mattie's other two employees, Edith and Abigail.

"We heard a scream and came running," Edith said. "Is everything okay? Was someone attacked? Robbed? Assaulted? Ambushed?"

"No, no, no, and no." So much for sneaking in when no one was watching. Maybe if she sat here long enough, someone would call the TV station and she could finish this up on the six-o'clock news. "I tripped. That's all. Nothing to worry about."

"Oh, dear," Abigail murmured.

"Oh, my," Edith echoed.

They hovered, like hens, fussing over her scraped palms and scuffed elbows. She tried her best to wave them away, hoping to hustle everyone back inside before her secret was discovered.

Though both Edith and Abigail were nearing eighty, neither dressed like little old women. Abigail hid her deceptively small and seemingly frail frame beneath a maroon wind suit. Her tiny, elfish face bore the deep wrinkles of a woman who'd smoked two packs a day for over thirty years. She'd needed something to keep her busy after giving up cigarettes in her sixties, so she'd become a born-again fitness junkie.

Edith, large boned and well padded, wore jeans and a plaid flannel shirt. The cortisone she took for her arthritis lent her features a puffy, pleasingly plump look. Despite her grandmotherly appearance, Edith took a gruff, no-nonsense approach to life.

As dear as Edith, Abigail and Lucy were to her, they tended to be nosy and overprotective. Today especially, she didn't want to stir their interest.

"I'm fine," Mattie insisted, a little more harshly than

necessary. "Go back inside. We're supposed to open in a couple of minutes. I'll pick up here."

Edith frowned. "Well, if you're sure you don't need help here, I'll get out the first-aid kit."

Abigail brightened a little. "I'll make tea. After all, it takes more than a kind heart to heal the wounds of the flesh."

Mattie stared at Abigail for a second, then shook her head. A year ago, Abigail had started taking tai chi, which she claimed had brought her greater spiritual enlightenment. Now every other sentence out of her mouth sounded like something straight from a fortune cookie.

"Yes, good idea," Mattie finally said. "Now—"

"Hey," Lucy interrupted. "What's the Kama Sutra?"

Instant silence. Three heads whipped around to face Lucy. Lucy had somehow made it down to her knees and was holding the incriminating book in both hands, staring at the cover in confusion. Slowly, Edith and Abigail—eyes wide and eyebrows raised—turned to Mattie.

Lucy looked up. "What?"

Great. Just great. How had she managed to hire what had to be the only nineteen-year-old in Northern California who'd never heard of the Kama Sutra and the only two eighty-year-olds who apparently had?

She struggled to her feet, then reached for the book with one hand and pulled Lucy to her feet with the other. "It's nothing. Just a library book I checked out. By accident. Just a silly mistake."

Now that was the understatement of the century.

"A silly mistake, my behind," Edith cackled. *"The Kama Sutra. The Joy of Sex. Dating for Dummies. The Multi-Orgasmic Couple. The Girlfriend's Guide to Great Sex."* Edith pointed to each of the books as she listed off the titles.

Picking up the books, Mattie said, "This is my business. My personal, private business."

"Poppycock." Edith stood, hands on her generous hips, blocking the door. "If you wanted this to be private, you wouldn't have brought those books here."

Abigail, all but wringing her frail hands, chimed in. "Edith is right, dear. Something must be terribly wrong. Bringing all those books about sex here is practically a cry for help."

"Omigod!" Lucy gasped. "You've decided to become a prostitute."

Mattie recovered her voice first. "What?"

Lucy stared back at them all, then shrugged. "Well, we all know you need money and with all these books about sex..."

"That's the conclusion you came to? That I'd decided to become a prostitute?"

Rubbing one hand over her swollen stomach, Lucy shifted nervously, then looked away. "Well, it's what Brooke on *Life's Golden Moment* did when she needed money."

"This is ridiculous." Mattie swung her purse strap over her shoulder and marched toward the door.

However, Edith stood her ground.

"What?" Mattie demanded. "Have you all gone insane? Is this the onset of senility? Surely you don't think I'm going to start walking the streets."

"Of course not." Edith crossed her arms beneath her heavy bosom. "But I smell a rat and I refuse to let you go hide in the office without telling us what's going on."

"Dear, we only want to help," Abigail chimed in.

"Yeah," added Lucy.

Sure they did. They weren't hens. They were vultures.

For the first time since she'd taken over the store, she found herself wishing she had normal employees. Employees she could boss around. Employees who minded their own business.

Mattie stared at them, one by one, hoping they'd waver. Abigail, who'd sat with her in the hospital during those last hard weeks before her grandmother passed away. Edith, who'd helped her research divorce lawyers and bullied her into choosing one. And Lucy...poor, sweet Lucy. She'd been one of Mattie's students her first year as a teacher. At twelve she'd been sweet, vulnerable, and already built like a Vegas showgirl. Frankly, Mattie was surprised Lucy had managed to stay out of trouble as long as she had.

They weren't just her employees; they were her friends. Practically her family. How in the world could she tell them to butt out?

Finally it was Edith's steely glare that wore her down.

"Okay, fine. I'll tell you everything. But let's just go

inside, so Lucy can get off her feet, Abigail can get her tea, and I can put these books down. They're heavy."

Edith eyed her opponent for signs of deception. At last, she stepped aside. "After you, boss."

"Humph," Mattie muttered as she walked through the door. Boss? That was rich.

Today she found no comfort in the things that normally soothed her at work—the rows and rows of brightly colored fabric, neatly arranged in Roy G. Biv order, the pungent scents of Abigail's Earl Grey tea mixed with Lucy's peppermint, the crisp smell of starched and sized fabric, and the cheerful, butter-yellow walls, hung with quilts made here at the store.

"We're waiting."

Fearing their reaction if they knew the whole truth, she skimmed over many of the pertinent details as she explained about Jessica's impromptu trip to Sweden, Brad's nasty ex, and his expertise in the area of small-business rescue.

"So, you see, it's really quite simple." Despite Mattie's reassurances, three pairs of doubtful eyes stared back at her. "He's going to help the store, and in exchange, I'm going to give him advice about his relationships."

"Oh, dear." Abigail cast a worried glance at Edith, then took a sip of tea.

Edith peered at her through narrowed, shrewd eyes. "What kind of advice? Advice about sex?"

"What?" It took her a moment to see the conclusion Edith had jumped to based on the books now tucked away in her office. She managed to stifle her laughter.

Barely. "Oh, no. I think I can safely say that the one thing Brad does not need advice about is sex. I'm just giving him advice about women and relationships."

Edith's eyebrows merged into a solid line across her forehead. "You're in way over your head, missy."

"I am not in over my head. I know exactly what I'm doing."

"Let me see if I've got this straight," Lucy said. "You've been in love with Brad for years—"

Mattie bristled. "How did you know that?"

Lucy winced, looking embarrassed. "Jessica told me."

"She what?" Oh, when Jessica got back from Sweden, they were going to have words about this.

Lucy just ignored her. "So this guy you've been in love with for years is back in town for just two weeks, he's living at your house, and you think this is a good idea?"

"Look," she said. "I've had a crush on Brad since I was ten. Let's face it, unrequited love has not been good to me. All my life, I've had this fantasy that Brad was the perfect man for me. Spending time with him is the only way to debunk the fantasies." She carefully avoided mentioning her plan to sleep with him. Somehow, she didn't think that would fly with this crowd. "Trust me. I know what I'm doing."

They still didn't look convinced.

"But, dear," Abigail asked, "what if you fall in love with him again?"

"I'm not going to fall in love with him. All I have to do is remain emotionally detached and I'll be fine. Besides, he's here for less than two weeks. No one falls in love in less than two weeks."

Edith frowned. "We're just worried about you, that's all. You don't have the best judgment when it comes to men."

Mattie bristled. "I am an excellent judge of character."

Edith snorted. "You're too trusting. Look at how Mike treated you."

"This situation is nothing like my marriage to Mike. For starters, I'm not going to let him anywhere near my finances. Besides, I've got it all planned out." She only wished she felt half as confident as she sounded. "As long as I stick to the path, I'll be fine."

"Even a very crooked path seems straight to a creature the size of a mouse," Abigail muttered.

Mattie frowned. "Am I the mouse in that analogy?"

"Dear, we're all mice when faced with insurmountable problems."

"Humph," Edith grunted. "Just don't get caught in your own trap."

9

DID PEOPLE ACTUALLY DO these things?

Mattie stared in fascination at a pen-and-ink drawing of a man with his arms stretched above his head and his hands tied to the headboard with a handkerchief.

The drawings intrigued her. Sex with Mike had been...uninspired. And for the first time, she regretted that.

Oh, she didn't blame him. Not just him, anyway. She hadn't done much to spice up their marriage, either. But now she found herself wishing she'd tried something a little different while she'd had the chance.

What about Brad? a niggling little voice in the back of her mind asked. If she ever got Brad into bed, would she need such tricks to keep things interesting? Or would merely being with him be enough? She suspected the latter.

After all, she had a lot of sexual frustration to work out. After years of anticipation, she wouldn't need anything kinky to keep her interested—all she needed was him in her bed. All that gorgeous naked flesh of his at her mercy. Just his skin against hers. His mouth, his body, his touch giving her pleasure.

Still, after they'd been together a while, after he'd

satisfied her every need many times over, then maybe she'd be ready to try something a little more...exotic. She found herself smiling mischievously at the thought.

In Mattie's mind, he was the perfect lover. He knew exactly what she wanted. He would try anything. And everything he did was perfect. The Brad of her fantasies was always perfectly in tune with her needs. Perfectly erotic. Perfectly satisfying.

But fast on the heels of that thought was another.

Her smile dropped away. She sat up, snapping the book closed. She wasn't supposed to enjoy being with him. In reality, he wasn't supposed to be perfect. He was supposed to be a disappointment. That was the plan, wasn't it?

Feeling suddenly edgy, she stacked the books on the corner of her desk and shoved back her chair. Walking down the box-lined hall to the shop's front room, she braced herself for another inquisition. When she walked through the door to find the three hens firing off a round of questions at Brad, she had to force herself not to panic.

Dear God, how long had this *been going on?*

Edith, arms crossing her chest and looking for all the world like a schoolyard bully, was asking, "If you really are Jessica's brother, why haven't we seen you before now?"

Mattie rushed across the room to the main cutting table where Brad stood, hands hanging limply at his sides as if facing a firing squad. "That's enough, Edith."

Abigail and Lucy started guiltily at the sound of her voice, but Edith didn't release Brad from her steely glare until Mattie reached them and placed a hand on Edith's flannel-covered arm. "Of course he's really Jessica's brother. I grew up with him, remember?"

Edith met Mattie's pleading gaze. For a moment she simply studied her. Then her arms dropped to her sides and she stepped away. Walking past Brad to where the pieces of a double-wedding-ring quilt lay spread out across the table, she muttered, "Never hurts to be cautious. That's something we should all remember."

Mattie caught Brad's expression, then rolled her eyes. To Edith, she said, "Yes, yes. Caution is very good."

Edith turned back around. But before she could open her mouth, Mattie rushed on. "I could really use a cup of coffee and I'm sure you all—" she stared pointedly at her friends "—have work to do getting this quilt ready for tonight's class."

She didn't dare wait for an answer. Who knew what those three would come up with next? Instead, she grabbed Brad's arm and headed for the door.

"There's a coffee shop two doors down. We'll have a little more privacy there."

Once safely outside the shop, she shot him an assessing look. Gone was his casual *GQ* persona from yesterday. Today he looked every inch the businessman. Tailored pants, spiffy loafers and a blue oxford shirt that set off his eyes. She still held his arm, and the fabric beneath her fingertips had the feel of an elegant cotton-silk blend.

Suddenly very aware of the heat of his flesh beneath that shirt and of the tensing muscles under her fingers, her mind flashed back to how it had felt to be in his arms the night before. And then to how he'd looked that morning, tousled and sexy, straight from his bed. His bare chest tanned, his muscles toned, his jeans low on his hips.

Last night, she'd come so close to having him at her mercy. Then his damn standards got in the way. But he wanted her. She could see it in his eyes every time he looked at her. It was only a matter of time before she wore him down and got him exactly where she wanted him.

Convincing him to cast aside his noble intentions would take a nifty little bit of manipulation.

Luckily, her conversation this morning with Abigail, Edith and Lucy had given her an idea. Brad may not need advice about sex, but questioning his skills had always been the easiest way to bait him. If nothing else, it would force him to talk about sex. Which just might weaken his resolve.

She cast a sidelong glance in his direction.

For the first time in their relationship, she held a decent hand of cards. True, not a royal flush, but she still had the advantage. Brad had tipped his hand. She now knew he wanted her. With that little ace, she'd be able to bluff her way to a winning hand.

SHE WAS STILL contemplating how best to play her cards a few minutes later when they settled into a

booth by the front window of Cutie Pies. Their waitress, who'd eyed Brad appreciatively while taking
their order, flounced off with an exaggerated swish of
her hips.

Before she could bring up the subject of sex, he
reached into his breast pocket and withdrew a small
leather-bound portfolio. He flipped it open, doubling
the cover back on itself, and pulled out a pen.

"Before we do any serious work, I'll need to take a
look at your books."

She blinked in surprise. "Excuse me?" she squeaked.

How had he known about the books? Had one of the
three hens told him?

He looked up at her, a frown marring his forehead.
"Your books. Your financial records."

"Ooh." She sank back against the booth in relief.
"My books. I thought you meant—" She laughed, wav-
ing a hand. Apparently, he didn't have sex on the brain
the way she did. She'd have to work on that. But she'd
let him get this business stuff out of the way first.
"Well, never mind. My financial records. Yes, you can
look at those."

His frown deepened, giving her the impression he
didn't think she was taking this seriously enough.
"While I'm looking through those, you can put together some of the other things I'll need." After writing
something on the notepad, he tore out the top page.
"Normally, Denise would contact you a week prior to
our first meeting so you'd have time to get these documents in order. Since we're working on a tight sched-

ule here, I'll just look over these as soon as you get them to me."

She took the page he held out and studied it. "Business plan. Mission statement. Employee records, including but not limited to employee evaluations and salary information for the last five years..." Hmm. He was taking this awfully seriously. Of course, he didn't know she had asked for his advice about her shop merely as a ploy to keep him in Palo Verde long enough to get him into bed.

Nevertheless, she had to admire his single-mindedness. Would he be this intense in bed? So totally focused on the task at hand? Completely unwilling to be distracted by anything?

She itched to find out, but she never would unless she got him to let down his guard a little. Something he'd never do if he was off studying her books without her. "Brad, you've barely even seen the shop. Why do you need all this?"

"I've seen enough. Neither of us has time to waste with show-and-tell."

"Show-and-tell?" His callous words sent a little shiver of unease down her spine. "Spending a little time in my store, getting a feel for how we do business isn't what I'd call show-and-tell."

"Trust me, Mattie. I know what I'm doing."

They were words meant to inspire her confidence, but they were spoken without emotion. They were the words of a businessman. A man comfortable in spiffy loafers and expensive dress shirts.

And for the first time, Mattie was aware of the years

that had passed since she'd last seen Brad. Almost a decade. A decade could do a lot to a person. Could change a man into someone for whom money was everything and people's hopes and dreams were interchangeable and disposable. A man for whom she was nothing more than another client.

Suddenly the Brad who sat across from her seemed like a stranger. She was sure this Brad was very good at his job, but she wasn't sure she wanted his sticky little fingers anywhere near her store.

She leaned back to allow room for the waitress to set down their drinks. Again, he never looked at the waitress, but Mattie nodded in the girl's direction. Returning her attention to Brad, she said, "Tell me something, Brad. Is this what you do for all those other businesses you 'save'?"

"Yes. This is exactly what I do."

"You swoop in, study all their paperwork, all their records, and then you—" she made a give-me-more gesture with her hands "—and then you what?"

"I make recommendations based on what I've learned. Help them devise a more specific business plan and more efficient processes."

"And you do exactly the same thing for every business. Whether it's a four-employee quilt store or three-thousand employee computer company?"

"Most of my clients are somewhere in between, but yes, I do the same thing every time. Because it works." He took a sip of his coffee then leaned back.

Every inch of him radiated the aura of a confident

businessman. And frankly, his attitude irritated her. She was not interchangeable, damn it.

"Mattie, do you know what the problem is with most small businessmen?"

Just to annoy him, she asked, "The tall women they date can't wear high heels?"

He stared at her for a moment, nonplussed, then continued as if she hadn't spoken at all. "The problem with most small businessmen, and women, is that they're not businessmen. Their specialty is something else. They're someone with a good idea or a good technique, but without any training in business. That's what I provide—the business sense."

"You think I have no business sense?"

"You're a teacher, not a businesswoman. Your grandmother was a quilter, not a businesswoman."

"I'll have you know my grandmother was a damn good businesswoman."

"Then you shouldn't mind if I take a look at the documents I've requested."

Unwilling to admit that, other than the financial records, she didn't have any of the documents he'd requested, she balled the sheet of paper in her palm. "No."

He raised an eyebrow, "Then I can't help you."

"Yes, you can. And you will." She tossed the balled-up paper on the table and calmly sipped her hot cocoa. "But if you're going to help my business, you need to help *my* business. You need to spend time in my store. Get to know my employees and my customers. Then I'll let you give me advice. But I'm not going to sit here and listen to some spiel you memorized a decade ago in 'how to be a heartless businessman' school.''

"Mattie, you're being irrational."

"Am I? I don't think so. I don't think it's too much to ask for something personal. It's what I would expect from an old friend." She eyed him, seeing his dress shirt and demeanor in a different light. "Of course, you're different than you used to be."

"Of course I am. Hasn't that been obvious?"

"I didn't mean in a good way." He flinched, almost imperceptibly, at her words, but she didn't retract them. "I'm curious. Is this how you treated Ginger?"

Angling back into the booth, he stretched one arm along the top of the bench and left one hand beside his coffee mug, his fingers tapping out a frustrated tune. "How I treated my wife and how I'm treating your business are two completely different issues."

"Are they?" She leaned forward, bracing her elbows on either side of her mug and reaching for his hand. His fingers, warm and slightly roughened, seemed to dwarf hers. Her pulse kicked up a notch as she remembered these fingers had caressed her skin last night and driven her to distraction. "Look, I'm only trying to help."

His fingers contracted, wrapping around hers, and she felt some of the tension seep from him. "I don't see the connection."

"A woman likes to...no, *needs* to feel special. Unique. As if she is the only woman in the world that matters to you. You already admitted that your assistant bought

Christmas presents for your mom and Jessica. Did she shop for Ginger, too?"

He untangled his fingers from hers, took a sip of coffee and shrugged. "Denise has excellent taste. And she enjoyed shopping. She mentioned it several times. Besides, surely one woman knows what to buy another woman better than I would."

"'Another woman'? Ginger wasn't just some other woman. She was your wife. She needed to know you cared about her. You. Not Denise."

"I married her, didn't I?" Frustration and anger laced his voice. "Isn't that proof enough that I cared?"

"If it was, would you need my help?"

For a long moment, he simply studied her. She shifted restlessly under the scrutiny of his blue eyes. He smiled ruefully. "No, I suppose not." His smile faded and his gaze turned suddenly solemn. "Is that why our marriage ended? Because I wasn't affectionate enough?"

His words tugged at her heart and, for an instant, she saw him not as the attractive grown man he was— or even as the heartless businessman he tried so hard to seem—but as a child. A little boy, lonely and uncertain.

The surge of emotion she felt in that instant was dangerous. All this time she'd been telling herself she only lusted after him. Now she wasn't so sure. When had love gotten so much more complicated than sex?

She forced herself to answer his question. "I don't know." Determined to regain control of the conversation, she smiled brightly and said, "But I have a plan to help you figure out that very thing."

"You do?"

"Absolutely." She reached into her back pocket and pulled out the single sheet of notebook paper on which she'd earlier scribbled a few notes. She was careful not to let him look too closely at the page she held before her. "I've listed some areas where—as a husband—there may be some room for improvement."

"What's on the list?"

"Okay, first off—were you stingy with money?"

"Define stingy."

"Were you cheap? Did you nag her about her spending?"

"I don't think so, and no."

She nodded and made a great show of checking "stingy" off her list. "Okay, then. Did you criticize her cooking?"

"Ginger rarely cooked. But I used to complain that when she ordered Chinese takeout she'd get too many tofu dishes."

She finished off the last of her cocoa and gestured to the waitress for the bill. "Were you mean to her in public?"

"No." He sounded offended. Good for him.

"Did you get along with her parents?"

"Most of the time."

"Did you tell her she looked fat in her swimsuit?"

"No."

"Were you bad in bed?"

Surprise flickered across his face. Then he laughed. "Yeah, that must've been it."

Oh, he was making this almost too easy.

Ignoring his sarcasm, she folded the sheet of paper in half and slipped it into her front pocket. "Excellent. So that was the problem then. You're bad in bed."

BRAD'S SMILE FADED and his expression shifted to one of pure horror. He glanced nervously at the nearest table to see if the other patrons had overheard her. Apparently being bad in bed ranked even lower than being mean in public. "Mattie, I was being sarcastic."

She pretended to carefully consider his claim, then she shook her head, dismissing it. "No. I don't think you were. I think your sarcasm may have been hiding a deeper fear about your inadequacies in bed."

The waitress walked up with the bill just as the words "inadequacies in bed" left Mattie's mouth. Dropping the bill on the table, the girl's eyes widened as she gaped first at Brad, then at Mattie.

Brad leaned forward, ignoring the now-retreating waitress. In a low voice he said, "I don't have any inadequacies in bed."

Mattie smiled gamely. "Whatever."

"I don't."

"If you say so." She tossed some cash on the table. "Actually I was rather proud of you for having the courage to bring it up. Most men are too proud to admit they have a problem."

As coolly as she could, she grabbed her bag, slid out of the booth and headed for the door.

It took him a minute to catch up with her on the street. "Trust me, in bed was the one place Ginger and I didn't have problems."

She flashed him a condescending smile. "I'm sure you're right."

"I am right."

"Of course you are."

He stopped and grabbed her arm. Her forward momentum spun her around to face him and he grabbed her other arm, as well. "I know why you're doing this."

"You do?"

"Oh, yeah."

His hand was hot and firm on her arm. Just a few inches separated them, but it felt like too much space. She drew in a lungful of air, but even the extra oxygen couldn't combat her sudden light-headedness.

"You're trying to goad me."

"Goad you?" she asked innocently.

"Into proving I'm not bad in bed."

"I would never do something that underhanded," she insisted in her most indignant voice.

"Oh, yes you would." He tugged her closer and she could feel his warm breath on her face. "But it's not going to work."

His nearness was muddling her thoughts and it took her a second to scrounge for an appropriately sassy reply.

"Don't worry. I'll go easy on you. We can take it nice and slow and practice as often as you need."

His hands tightened on her arms and for an instant

she wondered if she'd pushed too hard. Then she saw the glint in his eyes.

No, she hadn't pushed too hard. She'd pushed exactly hard enough to snuff out the heartless businessman and free the real Brad—the Brad who'd never backed away from a challenge in his life.

"Nice try, Sprout, but I'm not going to take you to bed."

She placed her hand on his forearm and asked—in her most concerned voice, "Is this problem with physical intimacy a recent development or did it affect your relationship with Ginger, too?"

"Whatever problems Ginger and I had, I can guarantee sex wasn't on the list."

"Are you sure? Some women are very adept at faking it."

"Yeah, I'm sure." He dropped his voice to a low, husky growl. "Unless it's a bad thing when a woman screams so loud the neighbors call the police."

His words caressed her and she nearly whimpered in response. His touch softened as he stroked the sensitive skin of her inner arm with his fingertips. "Unless it's a bad thing when a woman comes so many times she can't catch her breath and almost passes out."

His words sent a shiver through her body as she remembered just how he'd touched her last night. Thinking on her feet had never been harder.

"Sounds like a neat trick, but it's a little hard to believe. You'll forgive me if I need proof."

"Last night wasn't proof enough?"

"I've been alone for a while now. I was probably a little...trigger-happy. That's hardly a fair test."

"Trigger-happy?" His smile broadened and he dropped her arms. He shoved his hands into his pockets. "Nice try."

"We're both consenting adults."

"And if I thought you could be even half as unemotional about this as you think you can, I'd strip you naked right now and make love to you here in the street."

He let his words hang in the air for a moment, giving her plenty of time to search for a witty comeback. Unfortunately, witty anything was completely beyond her capabilities.

Then he chucked her on the chin before stepping away from her. He sauntered over to his car, which was parked in front of A Stitch in Time. He opened the door, but before sliding inside he said, "Don't forget to get those documents for me by tomorrow."

"I am unemotional," she called out. "I'm like a robot. Or like Mr. Spock."

He flashed her another cocky grin. "Sure you are, Sprout."

As she watched him drive away, frustration settled over her. Sexual frustration for sure, but something else as well. Anger with herself, maybe, for losing control of the conversation. Brad had recovered her conversational fumble and run with it. He'd scored a touchdown before she'd even realized he'd stripped the ball.

She dusted the defeat off her hands and headed back to the store. Sure, he was ahead at the end of the first quarter, but the game was still up for grabs.

10

AS SHE SCROUNGED together the store's financial and employment records and saved the files onto a Zip disk, Mattie felt a bit like she had the time her grandmother caught her reading *Cosmo*'s "50 Tricks to Drive Him Wild." Nervous and a little ashamed, even though she hadn't really done anything wrong.

For someone struggling to be a strong, financially independent woman, she'd sure made some rotten decisions about money in her lifetime. Trusting another man with her finances terrified her, but Brad wasn't Mike. He wouldn't make the same mistakes Mike had. Besides, she'd only take his advice if she trusted it.

If there was any chance—any chance at all—that he could fish A Stitch in Time out of these economically troubled waters, shouldn't she let him? Which was more important, the store or her pride?

The store, obviously. Because it wasn't just the store that was at stake. It was the jobs and future happiness of Edith, Abigail and Lucy. Frankly, she didn't give a fig about quilts, quilting or fabrics. But her employees? She cared passionately about them. If putting herself in Brad's hands would help save their futures, then that's what she'd do.

When she made it back to the house with the Zip

disk and a cardboard box full of her grandma's primitive record keeping, she found Brad in the living room. He sat on the sofa, with his shoes cast aside, his feet propped on the coffee table, and his laptop in his lap. He had his cell phone pressed to his ear with one hand while he typed—hunt-and-peck style—with the other. When he glanced up and saw her standing in the doorway, he ended the conversation and closed the laptop.

"I couldn't find a lot of the stuff on that list, but here's what I did find." She gestured to the box. Then, feeling as if more needed to be said, she added, "Sorry I acted like a brat at the coffee shop."

He smiled. "No, you're not."

"Well." She planted her empty fist on her hip and pretended to consider it. "Maybe not. After all someone needs to keep your ego in check."

"I appreciate your efforts." He leaned forward to poke around in the box. "Okay. Give me a week, I'll look this over and write you a new business plan. I may stop by the store once or twice, but for the most part, you won't even know I'm there."

"And what about you?"

"What about me?"

"We have a deal, remember? Tit for tat. You've got my records. When do I get my hands on your—" she looked pointedly down at his lap "—whatever?"

BRAD'S BLOOD THRUMMED in response to Mattie's words. He should have known better than to try to have a conversation right now. He hadn't quite shaken off the aftereffects of their conversation this afternoon.

The little minx had tempted and teased him almost beyond his endurance. Even though he'd tried to bury himself in work, what he really wanted to bury himself in was her.

"Didn't we go over this already? As tempting as your offer is, I'm not taking you to bed for practice."

"We'll see about that." Turning on her heel, Mattie headed for the kitchen. He refused to let her have the last word, so he followed her. She stood by the sink, slicing open a bag of prewashed lettuce. "We had a deal. You give me advice about how to run my store. I give you advice about women. Just because you won't let me help you where you need it most, I'm not letting you back out."

He tried to muster some annoyance at her blatant stabs at his manhood, but found he couldn't. Her teasing was too playful, too reminiscent of their past and the way she had treated him as a teenager. Besides, she was just so damn cute when she was trying to bait him.

The other day in the park she'd said everyone needed a playmate—and he realized she was right. He had no one to play with in his life. No one who treated him with irreverence. No one who teased him.

Until she'd walked back into his life, he'd never noticed the gaping hole where fun had been.

He wanted her to fill that hole, and it scared the hell out of him. With so much keeping them apart, playing with her now was a temptation he needed to resist. But he couldn't.

He held up his hands in an I'm-innocent gesture. "I'm not trying to back out." He purposefully egged her on. "I'll still help you. I just don't want any help in return."

"So you want me to forget my end of the bargain," she pointed out as she tossed chunks of chicken and cheese onto the salad. "You want me to accept help from you without giving anything in return."

"Yes."

"No." She grabbed a tomato from the bowl on the counter and reached for a knife. "This is my business. I've worked for it, I've fought for it. And yes I want it to be a success, but I don't want something for nothing."

"So what are you saying? You won't accept my help unless I accept yours?"

"Exactly." After tossing most of the tomatoes on top of the salad, she popped one bite into her mouth, then licked the juice off her fingertips.

Lord, she was killing him and didn't even seem to notice.

"That's ridiculous."

"No. It's not." She mumbled the words around the bite of tomato then swallowed. "Would you give free advice to any of your other clients?"

"Of course not."

"Then don't give it to me. Knowing you're getting something in return will keep you honest. Make you work harder. Besides I don't want your charity."

"It wouldn't be—"

"Yes, it would." She grabbed a bottle of salad dressing from the fridge and headed for the table. "Grab that, will you?" She gestured toward the bowl of salad. "If you're doing work for me and I'm not paying or helping you in any way then it most certainly is charity. If I wanted charity, I could get it from my father or Jessica. And if I'm not willing to accept charity from either of them, you can bet I'm not willing to accept it from you."

"Fair enough." He couldn't help but admire her determination. Unfortunately, it made her even harder to resist.

Keeping his hands off her had become a game of wills. She was so damn tempting. Even just watching her move around the kitchen made him want her. She brought passion to everything she did and the more time he spent with her, the harder it was to imagine returning to his bland and staid life without her.

As she scooped some of the salad onto her dinner plate, she said, "Well, if you won't let me give you advice about sex, you've got to give me something else to work with. What else were you bad at as a husband?"

"I don't know."

"Come on, you've got to give me something, anything." Elbows propped on the table, she leaned forward, a mischievous smile on her face. "We could talk about your skills in bed again, but I don't think that's such a good idea since you're so obviously insecure about sex."

It'd be so damn easy to take her to bed and prove to her exactly how competent he was. But with her, he didn't feel like an accomplished lover. He felt more like the bumbling, brash teenage boy he'd been on that long-ago Thanksgiving day. Too eager. Too clumsy.

Too hard to even think straight. But hey, maybe enthusiasm would count for something.

The offer was almost too tempting, and he had to struggle to remember why he'd promised himself not to sleep with her. Suddenly, he wanted to shove the dinner plates aside and make love to her right here on the table.

Oh, he had it bad.

He needed to either get a handle on his thoughts or change the subject, fast. He forced out the first thing that came to mind. "Presents."

"What?" She paused, fork raised almost to her lips.

"Ginger always said I was rotten at giving gifts."

"Oh." She chewed slowly, looking thoughtful. "Well, that's easy enough. The problem was your gifts were generic. Good for any person on any occasion. Which is basically what happens when you have your secretary do your shopping. So if—"

"This was before Denise. When I did my own shopping."

She studied him for a long moment, then set down her fork. "So that's why you had Denise shop for you? Because you think you're bad at it?"

"I don't think I'm bad at it. I know I am. I never gave Ginger a single present she liked besides her two-carat engagement ring. And she helped pick that out."

"Wow, two carats? No wonder she liked it. Give me an example. What kind of presents did you give?"

He thought back to the early years of his marriage, back when he'd still been trying to please Ginger. "A tennis racket for her birthday."

"Did she play tennis?"

"She used to. But when I gave her the racket, she claimed I only gave it to her because I was tired of losing at doubles and wanted her to improve her game."

"Were you?"

"Tired of losing? Probably." He dropped his gaze to the empty dinner plate in front of him. "Was that my sole motive? I don't remember anymore." He only remembered the fight that had followed.

"Do you remember what kind of gifts Denise would buy for her?"

"Jewelry, days at the spa, that kind of thing."

Mattie leaned forward and put her hand on his arm. The gesture was unexpectedly tender. Even more unexpected was the surge of emotion he felt in response. He brought his eyes back to hers. Staring into her eyes, he felt the connection between them deepen inexplicably. He felt, not for the first time, as if the bond they shared was more powerful than he'd ever admitted.

"The gift thing is really hard," she murmured. "It takes a long time to get it right. Some men never do."

Feeling as drawn to her as ever, he leaned toward her, but she jerked away from him, yanking her hand from his arm.

She stared fixedly at the salad before her for a long moment, then finally said, "Maybe you were trying too hard."

"What?"

She poked at her salad with her fork. "With the gifts, I mean. The presents you—or rather Denise—bought Jessica were always so expensive. The diamond tennis bracelets. Or the cruise to the Caribbean for your mom. Maybe you need to think smaller."

"Smaller than a diamond tennis bracelet?"

"Not smaller in size. Smaller in budget. Something that shows you care, something thoughtful."

"I thought the Caribbean cruise did show I cared."

"No. It showed you're rich. Now, if you'd gone on the cruise with your mom, that would have shown you cared." She slapped the table with her palm. "That's it."

"Huh?"

"You should give the gift of yourself." When he stared at her blankly, she explained. "Instead of buying Jessica a tennis bracelet, why not come down for the weekend to play tennis with her? Instead of buying a woman a day at the spa, why not give her a massage yourself?"

"Because a professional masseuse will do a better job than I can."

"It's not about the quality of the massage, it's about showing a woman you care enough to spend time with her." She flashed him a smug smile. "Besides, you can learn to give a good massage."

ALL THIS TIME, she'd been telling herself her emotions weren't involved, telling herself this was just about sex. She'd been wrong.

Tonight, as he sat across from her at the table, trying to think of ways he'd failed as a husband, she'd thought it was just part of the game. Part of the one-upmanship they'd been playing for years. She'd meant to goad him with her teasing. But the longer he sat there thinking, with his strong fingers tapping the oak tabletop, forehead furrowed in concentration, eyes narrowed in thought, the more she realized how genuinely hurt he'd been by Ginger.

The light overhead shone down, highlighting the blond streaks in his hair. The edges of him blurred by the light, he appeared less larger than life. More real.

Until this instant all of her emotions for Brad—powerful, mixed-up and confused though they had been— were rooted in the past. Rooted in the heart of the girl she'd been and the boy she'd loved. But now she saw him as a man. A real man. Not a perfect man, but a flesh-and-blood one.

And that scared the bejesus out of her. Lust, she could have fought indefinitely. But this?

This complicated blend of emotions? She'd have to fight tooth and nail to keep this at bay. This was no longer just about putting to rest her teenage fantasies. This wasn't about protecting her heart. She realized now that was an impossibility. Instead, it was about giving herself something she'd always desired and helping Brad in the process.

Brad seemed to have forgotten the first rule of playing sports—every team you played against was unique. One needed a different strategy and defense for every game. If she could teach him that, he'd be fine on his own once he went back to San Francisco. All she had to worry about now was her own defense.

"You're crazy. You do realize that, don't you?"

Mattie looked up from the "Art of Massage" pamphlet she'd received free with the purchase of her massage oil.

"Shh," she said, trying—not very successfully—to keep her lips from twitching. "I'm concentrating."

She pretended to return her attention to the booklet but surreptitiously studied Brad instead.

"Enough already." Brad abandoned his stance by the kitchen stool and crossed to stand over her where she sat on the kitchen table, bare feet dangling just above where Avenue lay sleeping under the table. "Let's get on with this."

Trying not to notice how close his thigh was to her bare knee, she quipped, "Patience is still a virtue." She waved him back to the stool. "You can't rush a sensual massage."

He glowered but still went to stand in the middle of the kitchen behind the inflatable doll that sat perched on the stool.

Naturally, Mattie had offered to be on the receiving end of this massage. The look of sheer terror on his face at her suggestion had been worth her earlier trip to the adult bookstore for the massage oil. In the end, they'd compromised. He'd agreed to practice massage—just not on her.

"Okay." Mattie tried her damnedest to keep the laughter from her voice, but if the look Brad shot her was any indication, she hadn't succeeded. "First you should rub your palms together to warm the oil so you don't shock her with the cold."

Brad picked up the bright red bottle and squirted some liquid on his palms. He didn't rub his hands together, but applied them directly to the back of the doll.

"If Suzie here was a real woman, you'd have just lost her trust." Mattie glanced down and read from the booklet. "'The oil should be body temperature and the first touch gentle. You're trying to establish trust.'"

Brad ran his hands up to the doll's shoulders. "If Suzie here were a real woman, she wouldn't have to be tied to the chair so she wouldn't float away."

Mattie shrugged. "Sorry. All we had at the store was the helium tank."

His head whipped around. "You blew her up at the store?"

"She'd take too long to inflate by hand."

"What about the little old ladies? What are their names?"

"Edith and Abigail."

"Right. They didn't have heart attacks when they saw you inflating a sex toy, did they?"

"Actually, they thought it was a hoot. However, in Suzie's defense, she's not a sex toy. She's a novelty item." Mattie picked up Suzie's plastic wrapper and pointed to the words printed on the label.

"All sex toys say that. It's a legality."

Mattie shook her head. "I think in Suzie's case it's true. Notice she doesn't have any—" Mattie pointed to the doll's painted bow mouth "—orifices."

Brad twisted the doll's head around so he could see her face. He nodded. "Good point."

"You know, if she were a real woman—" she began.

Brad cut her off. "If she were a real woman, you wouldn't be here giving instructions."

The reminder that he'd soon be leaving her life made her stomach flip over with a sickening thud. To hide her reaction, she stuck her tongue out at him. He laughed.

"'Step two,'" Mattie read from the booklet. "'Run your hands from the nape of her neck down the length of her spine.'"

She looked up in time to see Brad give her a hard stare before turning his attention to the doll. He clenched his hand on her neck and her head bobbed to one side.

"Run your fingers down her neck. You're trying to turn her on, not strangle her."

"This is harder than it looks." He loosened his grip and her head bobbed back into place. "She's flexible."

"Most men like that in a woman."

He glared at her.

"Just be gentle."

"You want to give this a try?"

"Oh, no. I know how to give a massage."

"Really? What makes you such an expert?" He looked up from the task at hand. "That ex of yours—what was his name?"

"Mike."

"Right. Was Mike into giving massages?"

"Not to me, he wasn't. But I'd have to ask his girl-friends to know for sure."

Brad's fingers tightened around the doll's neck and her head nodded forward. "Mattie, I'm sorry."

"Don't be," she said, her voice a little too cheerful. "Mike was into doing what was easy. If I hadn't made cheating easy for him, he wouldn't have done it."

"You can't blame yourself."

"I don't." She drifted into silence, staring at the words in the booklet without seeing them. Avenue snuffled and rolled over in her sleep.

Mattie shook her head and went on. "No, the massages were from Jessica. Last year for my birthday she gave gift certificates for monthly massages at the Wildflower Day Spa." The words tumbled from her mouth. Babbling like an idiot. That always makes a good impression.

She meant to shut up, but when Brad let go of the doll and rounded the stool toward her, she found another barrage of words escaping.

"I'm sure it was ridiculously expensive, but you know Jessica, no gift's too expensive, no purchase too extravagant. It must run in the family."

Brad took her face in his hands and tilted it up.

"Mike was an idiot."

His deep blue eyes met hers and she felt as if he were looking straight into her soul. She nodded. "I know he was. But I was the idiot who married him."

Brad shook his head. "You were young and in love."

"Yes, I was." Tears pricked at the backs of her eyes. What Brad didn't realize was that she'd been young and in love—with him. "That's no excuse."

"People have done stupider things for stupider reasons."

"Oh, I don't know about that."

Brad shrugged, leaning closer. "Mike was stupid enough to let you go."

His focus dropped to her lips and she realized he was thinking about kissing her. For a flicker of a second, she allowed herself the fantasy of letting him kiss her again. Like a shot of adrenaline straight to the heart, excitement rushed through her.

She lifted her chin, raising her lips in anticipation. But instead of kissing her, he stepped back, cocked his head to the side as if listening, and asked, "What's that?"

"What?"

"That noise. What's that noise?"

My pulsing blood? My thundering heart? My rampant hormones singing "Zippity Doo Da"?

"What noise?" she choked out. "I don't hear anything."

But then she did. A faint *psssst* noise. A noise that sounded suspiciously like air escaping from a cheap novelty blowup item. She peeked around Brad's shoulder.

Suzie slumped forward, her head bobbing to her knees as the helium seeped out, her foot caught firmly in Avenue's mouth. Suddenly the center of attention, Avenue barked guiltily, then skulked off to the back door.

"Oh, no," Mattie murmured, staring at the deflated Suzie. "We've killed her."

11

"GUESS THE LESSON'S OVER," Brad said, relief obvious in his voice.

"What do you mean the lesson's over? It's not over."

Brad pointed to the now-limp doll. "Suzie deflated. Didn't you notice?" He smiled as he lifted Suzie's hand then let it drop to her side.

"No way. You're not getting out of this that easily."

"This is easily?"

She jammed her fists on her hips and squared off against him. "I promised to teach you how to give a massage and I'm gonna do it."

"You're only making this harder on both of us. Why are you being so bullheaded about this?"

"It's—" She hesitated. For an instant, she considered spilling her guts, but she didn't want to reveal she'd been pining for him all these years. "It's my duty."

He stiffened. "Is that how you see me? As some sort of charity project?"

"Isn't that how you see *me?*" She sighed, shaking her head slowly. "Look, if either of us is going to make any progress, we have to trust each other. We have to stop trying to outmaneuver one another."

He shot her a look from under his lashes. "Maybe."

"There's no maybe about it. I can help you, Brad."

"Neither of us needs the kind of help you're offering."

"Look, I know I've given you a hard time about being bad in bed. But forget about that for a minute. You could be Don Juan in bed and you'd still have problems with women."

"Gee, thanks."

"You'd still have a grumpy assistant and unhappy dog trainer. You'd still worry about making mistakes the next time around. But I can help you. If you'll just let me."

"But you shouldn't have to."

"Why? Why shouldn't I have to? Because Brad Sumners—the perfect Brad Sumners, who never loses—isn't supposed to need help? Because you don't want to seem weak or vulnerable?" He stared at her for a long moment but said nothing. She didn't know whether or not to take his silence as agreement. She went on. "Look at it this way. I'm your secret weapon."

His eyebrows shot up. "My secret weapon?"

"Yes. Exactly." She warmed to the idea. "Remember back in high school, when there was that really big game against the West Coast Wombats or whatever they were called?"

"You mean the state championship. Against the Bay Area Badgers."

"Yeah, wombats, badgers, whatever. Do you remember that big pep rally they had before the game?"

"What about it?"

"My dad went on and on about how we were going to win—not only because our team was better, not only because we had the better, stronger, faster players. He'd been working all season on this new playbook and it was our secret weapon. It gave us an edge no other team had."

"How do you remember all this?"

"Do you have any idea how many times he practiced that speech? The point is, I can be your playbook." She took his hand and drew a tiny circle in his palm. "Your secret weapon. The inside information."

"I still don't follow."

She continued to gently rake her fingernails across the sensitive skin of his hand. "Dating, sex, love. It's all like one big state-championship game. You're on one team." She linked her fingers with his. "All the eligible women are on the other team. And the only thing better than having a really great playbook of your own would be to have their playbook, too." She studied Brad for a moment in the half-light of the setting sun. She hadn't convinced him. Yet. "I can be that for you. I can let you see the other team's playbook."

"We're talking about women, Mattie. Not football."

She turned to face him, then tucked a piece of hair behind his ear. "True, but it's still a game. Do you want to win or not?" she said softly, hoping the extra enunciation lent a seductive air to her words.

And with that, she knew she had him. Of course Brad wanted to win. He always wanted to win.

He made no attempt to move away from her, no attempt to remove her hand from his hair. Instead, he took a deep breath and said, "I'm still not going to bed with you. It'd be a mistake."

Unfazed by his constant litany of rejection, she smiled wryly. "I'll try to contain my disappointment."

Oh, he kept saying he wasn't going to sleep with her, but she was wearing him down. She could see it in his eyes.

"Besides, we're both adults. I can control myself if you can." Not that she actually intended to control herself. If she could tease him beyond his endurance, there'd be no need.

"Sure, I can control myself." He smiled, and she got the distinct impression that his levels of endurance just might be more than she'd bargained for. "What exactly did you have in mind?"

"I thought you could give me a massage. Unless, of course, that would be too great a test of your control."

"No," he said, perhaps too quickly. "Because, as you said, we're both adults. We can control ourselves."

"Exactly. So it won't be hard." She eyed him up and down. "Will it?"

He cleared his throat. "Not at all."

"Excellent. Because I think a massage would be the perfect way to relax." She stretched her arms over her head, very aware of her T-shirt rising up to bare her belly. Very pleased when she saw his attention drop to the gap between the hem of her T-shirt and her jeans. "It'll really help me get a good night's sleep. 'Cause after a massage, I always feel very—" she slowed the rhythm of her words "—sleepy."

His jaw went slack. *Gotcha.*

She took a moment to gather her courage and mentally apologize for the lie. Control herself? Who was she kidding? She couldn't even control herself on the kitchen counter while he was drunk and more than likely not at his best. She mentally crossed her fingers and hoped that in the midst of her inevitable loss of control, he'd be right there with her.

With a deliberately slow pace, she stood and crossed the room, then turned and crooked her finger in his direction. Part of her expected him to laugh out loud at her blatant come-on. Instead, he stood and gave her a cautious look. The rest of her brimmed with pleasure when, instead of laughing, he stumbled back a step.

"You—" he cleared his throat "—really want to do this?"

Her lips curved into a smile. "I'm game if you are."

WHY YOU LITTLE LIAR.

Brad watched her pause in the doorway. For all her bravado, Mattie was shaking in her boots.

Oh, she put on a good show. But he could read her better than she thought he could. Because beneath her bravado, beneath her carefully calculated sensuality, and even beneath her glimmer of self-confidence, she hid a tiny kernel of trepidation.

So, she could control herself if he could?

Just how far was she willing to go to prove her point?

Looking up at him through her lashes, she asked, "Where do you want me?"

Pretty damn far, it seemed. Where did he want her? Anywhere. Everywhere.

She blinked innocently. "Do you want me sitting on

the chair? Or lying down on the sofa? Or right here on the floor in front of the fireplace?"

Images flashed through his mind. Images of Mattie naked and willing shot through his head. Mattie poised on the edge of a chair, back arched, beckoning him to her. Mattie lounging on the sofa, hair spread out across a pillow, breasts proudly thrust upward, one leg bent at the knee. And of her spread out before him on the floor, propped up on her elbows, smiling up at him, welcoming him beside her.

"On the floor." He barely choked out the words.

"Good choice." Her lips curved into a seductive smile. She moved to the table and picked up the massage oil.

For a moment, he stared in silence at the bottle. Then it hit him. They were talking about the massage. Of course they were still talking about the massage. How had that gotten so muddled in his mind?

Because he hadn't had sex in over nine months, that's how. It had nothing to do with the fact that in the past several minutes, sweet little Mattie Wilcox had transformed into a sex goddess. It had nothing to do with the fact that the woman he'd sworn to keep his hands off despite his pulse-pounding fantasies had just somehow tricked him into putting his hands all over her.

Nope. Nothing at all.

He could do this. He could touch Mattie without this getting out of control. No problem.

He grabbed the bottle of massage oil from her outstretched hand, hoping to call her bluff before they ended up doing something they'd both regret. "You know what's even better than the floor?"

Her self-satisfied smile slipped from her lips. "No. What?"

"A bed. A nice comfy bed. Then you can really relax."

She blanched. But he had to hand it to her, she recovered quickly. "Sounds great."

Before he could stop her, she turned and headed for her bedroom.

Damn, but she was stubborn. He hadn't remembered her being so stubborn. Of course, as appealing as she'd been at fifteen, he sure as hell hadn't remembered her being this kick-in-the-gut sexy.

"You coming?" she asked over her shoulder. The challenge in her eyes was clear. If he backed down now, she'd peg him as a coward. And she'd know exactly how strongly she affected him.

What could he do but pick up the gauntlet she so brazenly tossed at his feet?

And even if he had thought better of it, he found himself stumbling mindlessly after her, as if his feet had automatically vetoed whatever judgment his brain might make.

"You couldn't keep me away."

Her smile shifted, then broadened. "I wouldn't expect anything else."

She ambled down the hall, the sway of her hips snagging his attention like a hypnotist's watch. He followed, filled with warring fascination and dread as she slipped into her bedroom. Pausing at the doorway, he watched as she slunk across the room.

Instead of turning on the overhead light, she slid open the top drawer of her dresser and pulled out a book of matches. Now armed, she moved around the room, lighting a scattering of candles on first one dresser and then the next before ending up at the bedside table where she lit a final fat pillar.

He was about to comment on the inexplicable attachment women seemed to have to what could only be considered a fire hazard, but before he could, she knelt on the bed, her back to him.

His sarcastic comment caught in his throat, unspoken, as he watched her grab the hem of her T-shirt and pull it up and over her head.

His thoughts fled fast on the heels of his words as he took in the pale expanse of her skin, broken only by the flesh-colored straps of her bra. Then she reached behind her and, with a flick of her fingers, unlatched that as well. With a deft and surprisingly agile movement, she shimmied her arms free of the straps and tossed it on the floor. Then, with her arms crossed over her chest and her hands resting on her shoulders, she half turned to face him. The curve of her breasts, full and lush, was visible beneath her arm.

Desire hit him hard in the stomach, but he did his best to knock it back. This game they were playing was about one-upmanship, not sex. Mattie was just toying with him, not because she was cruel or heartless but because she was proving her point.

This act of brazen sensuality was no different than

the confidence she had feigned when she walked away from their unexpected kiss by the pool. Of course, that act had stirred his admiration; this stirred something else entirely. Now it wasn't her courage he admired, but her other...assets. The sight of her moving to lie facedown on her bed filled him with the need to join her on the bed, strip off her remaining clothes and bury himself deep inside her.

Somehow he got his body—and his urges—back under control. If she could take this, then he could, too. So, massage oil and libido firmly in hand, he crossed over to her.

She propped her chin on the backs of her linked hands and eyed him from where she lay.

"You took your shirt off." *That's right, buddy, dazzle her with your intellect.*

Her lips twitched and she quirked an eyebrow. "Massaging the oil into my shirt would be a little messy."

"Right."

He stood motionless beside the bed for another long moment. Finally she took pity on him and said, "Don't tell me you've never given a massage before."

"I..." He searched his memory. Freshman year in college he'd rubbed the shoulders of a girl in his physics study group. The girl had been fully clothed at the time. She'd been nearly fully clothed a few minutes later when they'd ended up having sex on her dormroom floor. Somehow he didn't think Mattie would consider that prior experience. So he admitted, "No."

Her smile broadened. "Well, you'll need to start by sitting down on the bed." He must have hesitated, because she added, "Don't worry, I won't bite."

That's what he was afraid of.

12

AWKWARDLY, trying to hide his growing erection, Brad lowered himself to the bed beside her. His hip close to hers, he hitched his knee onto the bed, being careful not to let his jeans brush against her bare flesh.

"See there. That wasn't hard," she teased. "Now pour a little of the oil onto your hand—" She paused, watching him carefully as he followed her directions. "There. That's enough. Now rub your hands together to warm the oil. Then just rub it into my skin."

Following her instructions, he brusquely rubbed his hands together. The minty scent of the oil wafted up to him, flooding his senses. Her fresh floral scent mixed with the peppermint and the simple combination seemed more erotic than any of Ginger's expensive perfumes.

Closing his eyes, he drew in a deep breath and gave himself free rein to do what his body had been urging him to do ever since he first saw Mattie wrapped in that lemon-yellow towel. He touched her. Trailing his hands across her naked flesh, he explored the velvety skin at the back of her neck and the elegant hollow behind each of her ears.

He ran his hands down the slope of her neck and around the ball of each shoulder, then back to her spine. The delicate bones of her spine rose gently above the landscape of her back and he explored each of them with the tips of his fingers. Resting the balls of his hands against her lateral muscles, he rotated his hands, grazing his fingertips across her back in delicate arcs.

A low, feminine moan resonated through the room. Heat flooded his groin, tightening his erection. He jerked his hands away, squeezing his eyes closed and fighting to regain the control he felt slipping through his fingers.

"Too rough?" he asked.

"No." She sounded winded. "Not at all."

Almost of their own volition, his hands returned to their task. The oil made the exploration of her skin effortless but did little to diminish the heady heat of her body. His thumbs moved in ever-widening circles down to the small of her back, then to the edge of her denim shorts, with each stroke dipping under the denim waistband. The muscles of her back tightened, twitching almost imperceptibly beneath his touch.

"Is this okay?" He repeated the movement.

"Fine."

Lessening the pressure of his hands, he asked, "Too firm?"

"No. Firm is good."

"Too gentle?"

"Gentle is good, too."

Her voice sounded tight, as if it took all her effort to choke out the words. As if she, too, felt the strain of their proximity. The thought gave him little comfort.

Wanting Mattie was bad enough. Knowing she wanted him just as badly was torture.

Again she moaned and the sound tore through him, ratcheting his desire up another notch. He stifled a moan of his own.

"This is good," she murmured.

"This spot?" he asked, circling back to the patch of skin he'd just been lavishing with attention. "Or this pressure?"

"Neither. I mean, this is good. You asking questions."

"I have to ask. I've never done this before."

"Hmm. There's a thought. If you'd never been with a woman before, would you ask a woman what she liked or didn't like?"

"That's different."

"How?"

"It just is."

"But it shouldn't be. Every woman is unique. Being with other women doesn't necessarily prepare you for being with whatever woman you're with. So you ask her what she likes. What she doesn't like. Where she wants your hands. Where she wants your mouth. It's important for you to know what she wants."

His hands made their way up her back to her shoulder blades. He massaged first the tender muscles along her spine and then slowly worked his hands into wider and wider circles across her back, grazing her sides with his fingertips.

The feel of her skin beneath his hands was driving him crazy. In that moment, he'd never wanted anything more in his life than to turn her over and finish what they'd started. And for an instant, he considered doing it.

"What about you?" he asked.

"What about me?"

"What do you like?"

The question slipped out before he could stop it, and suddenly, she rolled over beneath him. Her breasts were firm and proud, her nipples tightening with desire. Her expression was filled with emotion, and darkened as he watched her.

SHE LAY BENEATH HIM, bare and vulnerable. Exposed.

The hunger in his expression matched her own. They'd played long enough; it was time to call his bluff. To put her own cards on the table.

"Damn it, Brad," she snapped, her frustrated desire making her terse. "If you're going to kiss me, then do it now. Otherwise, just leave. Or stop looking at me like that. Because you're driving me crazy."

A long moment of silence followed in which her heart beat so hard she was sure it would pop right out of her chest. He wasn't going to kiss her. She'd gambled and lost. Again.

"Never mind. Forget it." She wiggled out from under him and made straight for her shirt where it lay discarded on the floor. As she forced her arms through the holes, she turned back around to face him.

He sat on the edge of the bed, his head buried in his hands. Once again she was struck by the realization that he was not the perfect lover of her fantasies, but a flesh-and-blood man. Real, human and flawed. As vulnerable to her as she was to him.

He was not perfect, but perfect for her. Perfectly sexy, but also perfectly strong and perfectly stubborn.

As she looked at him, her chest tightened. "You should have given in. We would have been good together. And we both could have won."

She didn't wait to hear his reply, but moved to her dresser where she snuffed out the flames of the candles one by one. If only she could extinguish her desire as easily.

Then she felt his hand on her arm. Wordlessly he spun her around, pressed her to the wall beside her dresser and covered her mouth with his. The kiss seared her soul, reaching for and claiming parts of her that she hadn't even known existed. With his hands cupping either side of her face and his body crowding hers, she gave herself over to sensation.

For a moment her hands fluttered uselessly at her sides. She'd never been kissed like this. Mike had never kissed her like this. Even Brad, the other night in the kitchen, hadn't kissed her with such pent-up passion.

She had no idea what one did with her hands when being kissed senseless. Fortunately for her, her hands did know. They clung. Clung to his waist where it began to V up toward all those wonderful muscles. Clung to the hard resistance of his back. Then fumbled with the cotton of his shirt and the leather of his belt, tugging and cursing at the barriers. Praying that he wouldn't stop kissing her. That he would never stop.

She nearly cursed when his lips left hers, fearful he would once again let his blasted morals get in the way. But his lips didn't stray far. Those perfect, magical lips of his blazed a trail up her jaw to the skin just below her ear. He lingered there, nuzzling and nipping with sharp teeth, smooth-as-silk lips and a jaw covered with sandpaper-rough stubble.

That spot under her ear was the epicenter of a shiver that coursed through her whole body and left her tingling and weak. His passion shook her. Humbled her. Part of her knew he might regret this in the morning, but she couldn't seem to stop herself, let alone him. Whatever portion of her brain controlled her moral center didn't control her hands or mouth. Or her legs, she realized, as his thigh slipped between hers and her leg snaked up the side of his, wrapping around it, pressing against the back of his knee. Urging him closer.

He groaned against her neck. One hand braced against the wall behind her. The other slipped down to her knee, skimming along the bare skin, inching up the fabric of her shorts. His hand lingered on her thigh, hitching it up so that her center pressed against his. She strained up, extending her foot to bring him closer and arching her neck to give him better access.

One arm eased around her waist, holding her tight against him. The other cupped her bottom. When he lifted her off her feet, her legs instinctively wrapped around his hips. He spun them around, walked a few steps and gently set her down on the bed, the coolness of the sheets beneath her was a startling contrast to her heated skin.

With his lips sealing in any protest she might make, he found the zipper on her shorts. Time seemed to stop, and she would have sworn she could hear the individual clicks as he released each tooth of the zipper. His fingertips skimmed over the sensitive skin of her belly, tracing the ridges of her hips before easing her shorts down her legs.

Once again, she tugged off her shirt, but this time her movements were sharp, jerky with unreleased desire. This was no smooth seduction, no teasing come-on. She was desperate. Needy. Frantic to feel his skin against hers. He drew back just long enough for her to cast the fabric aside, and then his mouth was trailing kisses over the crests of her breasts, but refraining from meeting her nipples.

Returning to her mouth, his lips branded hers as his hands slid up her legs. She groaned her impatience, but still he teased, his thumbs tracing spirals over her inner thighs. She raised her hips, unconsciously urging him to rid her of her panties. Finally he pulled them off and his fingers sought her very center. He dipped into her, finding her moist heat, before withdrawing to circle the nub of flesh just above.

Reflexively she bucked against his hand. Her world contracted to only him. To only the feel of his fingers driving her to distraction, of his erection pressing against her hip, of his strength sheltering her from the storm of her reaction.

He urged her closer to release, drove her further

from sanity. Relentless and unforgiving, his fingers sought her orgasm, pushing her, demanding a response. His mouth left hers, trailed down her throat to her breast and seized her nipple. The nipple peaked within his mouth.

As close as she was, a part of her held back. He'd brought her here once before. He'd pushed her over the edge, but had refused to follow. She wouldn't let him do that again.

"No," she gasped.

Instantly his hand and his lips stilled. He groaned, pressing his forehead to her shoulder. "Mattie, this is a hell of a time to tell me no."

Struggling to contain her reaction to him, she ran her bare foot down the back of his thigh. Still, she nearly laughed at the sheer frustration in his voice.

With her arms and her legs wrapped around him, she rolled him onto his back. Sitting astride him, she grabbed both of his hands in hers and stretched them over his head.

She was completely naked. Though he was disheveled, he was still completely clothed. She'd have to do something about that.

She couldn't pull his clothes off him fast enough. She left his shirt half-undone to grope the zipper of his pants. She ached to explore every inch of his body. To immerse herself in him, to live out every fantasy she'd ever had. But the desire pulsing through her to just have him *now* drove her on.

His response fueled her passion. His fingers tore away his clothing just as frantically as hers did. His hands also shook as he pulled his shirt off and shucked his jeans. Before casting aside his pants, he yanked out his wallet and fumbled to pull out a condom.

Her hands itched to touch him, so she pulled the condom from him. She eased the condom down the length of his manhood, cradling him with her trembling fingers. He quickly lost patience. Long before her fascination was satisfied, he rolled her over on her back.

And then he was above her, kneeling between her spread legs. Easing into her, filling and completing her. With each thrust he reached deep within her, driving her closer and closer to release—driving her crazy. Then suddenly she was there, exploding outward and trembling to bring herself back in.

She clung to him as he thrust one last time, groaning out his orgasm. He kissed her gently, nuzzling at her throat, murmuring soft, sweet words of passion.

But not words of love.

13

"MISS MATTIE?"

Mattie cringed at the sound of Lucy's voice, then looked up to see the girl peeking sheepishly through the cracked door. "Just Mattie would be fine," she reminded her. Jeez, it had been bad enough when she'd been Lucy's teacher. Now it just made her feel like a castoff from *Gone with the Wind.*

"Mi—Mattie, can I talk to you?"

"Sure." She shoved aside the shipping manifest she'd been pretending to read and leaned back in her chair. "What's up?"

Lucy slipped through the door, cast a nervous glance back down the hall, then pulled the door closed behind her. "It's about Mr. Sumners."

"Yes?" Mattie prodded.

"I just... I mean... It—he makes me nervous. You're in here doing—" she waved her hand through the air "—whatever, instead of being out there where you'd normally be. And he's out there watching everything everyone does. But he keeps looking back here. Waiting for you to come out." Lucy's hands fluttered in front of her face as if she was swatting away gnats. Or tears. "And he just—"

Mattie stood and crossed to Lucy's side. "Honey, calm down."

Her hands stilled only when Mattie grasped them in her own. Then Lucy met her gaze. Soft brown eyes, glistening with emotions too close to the surface. "I just worry."

Mattie stroked the back of Lucy's hand. "Well, you shouldn't. He's here to help. I know he can be intimidating, but you have nothing to worry about. You know you'll always have a job here. I promise."

Lucy blinked in surprise, her tears clearing. "I'm not worried about my job. I'm worried about you!"

"Me?"

"Yes, you. I've seen the way you look at him."

Mattie jerked her hands away. "I don't know what you're talking about."

"You like him."

"Of course I like him." She shoved her hands into her pockets, hoping their tremble hadn't given away her lie. "He's Jessica's brother. What's not to like?"

"Oh, that's not what I mean." Again, Lucy's hands fluttered. "I mean, you...you act like your past with him means nothing, but it does. You're falling in love with him all over again."

"I'm not falling in love with him. I promise."

Lucy looked doubtful. To be honest, Mattie felt a little doubtful herself. Her feelings for him were almost too complicated to categorize. For Lucy's sake, she tried.

"Sure, I admire him. I appreciate his dry sense of humor. Even though it's frustrating to lose to him, I enjoy his fierce competitiveness. But I don't love him. I'm not stupid enough to let him break my heart."

Am I?

Lucy stamped her foot, obviously just as frustrated with the conversation as Mattie. "You're going to take him in like one of your strays."

"My strays? I don't take in strays. I don't have any pets."

"I don't mean stray pets. I mean stray people."

"Oookay," Mattie said. "You lost me again."

"If there's anyone in need, you want to help. You get suckered into people's lives. You try to take care of them. You take in needy people like other people take in stray cats."

"I do not." But she couldn't infuse much conviction into her words.

"Hellooo." Lucy gestured to her rounded belly. "Unemployable nineteen-year-old pregnant girl. You gave me a job—no questions asked—even though I have no skills. No—"

"Nonsense. You have plenty of skills. Remember what I've told you about self-esteem?"

Like the smart-alecky student she'd once been, Lucy rolled her eyes. "Yes, Miss Mattie, I do." Then she flashed back to the concerned young woman. "But I know what I am. And I know that if it wasn't for you I'd still be working the night shift at the Pac-N-Sac."

Mattie shifted uncomfortably. "I didn't do anything anyone else wouldn't have done."

"Yes, you did. You gave me a job. You helped me find an apartment when my mom kicked me out.

You've given me my future back. And that's what worries me." Lucy placed her hand on Mattie's arm. "If you've done all this for me, a student you hadn't seen in years, just because you felt sorry for me, then what will you do for Brad? The same Brad you used to be in love with?"

Unfortunately, Lucy wasn't the only one worried about that. That same concern had been niggling at the back of her mind ever since Brad had walked back into her life. Niggling at the back of her mind, consuming her every waking thought. Something like that.

Trying to reassure Lucy, she said, "Look, I'll be fine. Trust me."

Eventually, Lucy calmed down, but the conversation left Mattie with more than a few concerns of her own. She *was* too emotionally involved with Brad. And she didn't need Lucy to tell her that.

Making love with Brad last night had been everything she'd ever dreamed it would be. Quite a bit more, actually. More passionate, more earth-shattering, more emotional. Great sex she could handle, but the tug of emotions? Idiot that she was, she just hadn't been prepared for that.

And—if she were completely honest with herself— some tiny part of her clung to the hope he would choose to stay in Palo Verde.

It was ridiculous. She knew it was.

He hadn't loved her enough to stay in Palo Verde when he was eighteen. He certainly didn't love her enough now. Hell, forget whether or not he loved her *enough*. He didn't love her *at all*.

That thought sent a shaft of pain straight through her heart.

She'd tried so hard to throw up barriers against him. She'd tried so hard to protect her heart and in the end, it hadn't done any good.

Lucy was right. She was in serious danger of falling in love with him again. The only question was, what was she going to do about it?

"YOU WANT ME TO DO WHAT?" Brad wedged his shoulder against the arched doorway leading from the kitchen to the living room. The sleeves of his white shirt were rolled up to expose his forearms. His loosened tie hung just below his unbuttoned collar. He held a beer, apparently forgotten, in one hand, raised partway to his lips.

"I think you should go," she repeated, then sank back into the armchair, adjusted the fabric of the crazy quilt she was working on across her lap and made yet another clumsy stitch she'd later have to pull out. "You got whatever advice from me you needed, so now you should go back to San Francisco."

"What the—" He shook his head. He was—for once—at a loss for words.

For a long moment, Brad said nothing. Then, with stealth that stole her breath, he crossed the room. He braced his hands on the arms of the chair, trapping her. He leaned in close—so close she could smell the woodsy scent of his soap—and pinned her with a steady gaze.

"Is this what you want?" His eyes were filled with

questions and tinged with doubt. And maybe a little anger as well. "After last night, you want me to just walk away?"

His breath brushed against her cheek, against her mouth. It smelled sweet, fresh and faintly like the cinnamon mint she'd seen him pop in his mouth after lunch. She had to force herself to answer the question that hung in the air between them.

His nearness scattered her thoughts, preventing her from coming up with a coherent answer.

He inched closer, as if he could read her unspoken response in the depth of her eyes. "What is it you want?"

What did *she* want?

How long had it been since she'd thought about what she wanted? Months. Years maybe. Even longer since someone else had asked her.

The answer of course was simple. She wanted him— had always wanted him, for as long as she could remember.

She wanted the boy he'd been—fearless, confident and kind. But even more, she wanted the man he'd become—vulnerable, thoughtful and in desperate need of someone to play with.

With so much of her heart, she wanted to be his playmate. To make him laugh and to take away his sadness. But even more than that, she wanted him to take away hers.

She wanted him to love her, passionately. To desire her. Crave her. Need her, to the point of thoughtless unrestraint.

To feel the pulse and pull of her body every time he moved within reach of her, like the gravitational pull of one planet to another. As if his desire for her was the only thing keeping him from floating out into space.

Because that's how she felt about him.

And if he felt even a fraction of that attraction, he wouldn't be able to resist pulling her from the chair, pressing his body to hers and kissing her until neither of them could breathe.

Not that she could breathe now.

So she just sat, holding her breath, waiting, as the silence of the room settled around them. The very air seemed to tense, then relax, like a sigh.

She thought—imagined?—that his mouth moved closer to hers. Her eyes drifted closed, then flickered open at the scuffle of dog claws on the sliding-glass door.

Reality snapped back into place. She shot a glance toward the door, where Avenue sat waiting to be let outside. Brad straightened, stepping away from her so quickly he brushed against the coffee table.

He opened the door for the dog, then slid it closed behind her. Fisting one hand on his hip, he ran the other through his hair. "Is it?"

Her mind stumbled backward, searching for the lost thread of the conversation. "Is it what?"

"What you want me to do? To leave?"

She blinked, struggling to pull her thoughts together. "What does it matter?" she asked, her breath coming in a short burst of frustrated exasperation. Trying to gain a foothold, she stood and set aside the quilt she'd been mangling.

She felt defensive and panicky. Backed into a corner, she threw at him the only argument she had, even though it wasn't a particularly logical one. "This isn't about what I want. It's about you. About what you want. And your stupid deadline."

"My deadline? What the hell are you talking about?"

"You're going to leave anyway. Whether it's tomorrow or in two weeks, you're eventually going to leave. You're going to go back to San Francisco and—eventually—you're going to realize you really do want everything on the goal card of yours."

"I—"

"It'll just be easier on me if it happens sooner rather than later."

"You sure about this?"

"Positive. One hundred percent."

He reached out a hand as if to grasp her arm. "It doesn't have to be this way."

"Oh, yes, it does." She deftly stepped out of his reach, slipping behind the chair. She propped her hands on the back of the chair to hide the frustration trembling through them. "Let me ask you something about those goals of yours, Brad. Why were they so important to you?"

His gaze skittered away from hers and he rounded the coffee table and lowered himself to the sofa. He sagged against it, like a wounded man shifting his weight from a crutch.

Without meeting her eyes, he asked, "Have you ever been alone, Mattie?"

"Well, sure."

"I mean really alone. Cut off from everyone you know. Powerless."

As he assessed her, she could only shake her head. "No. I suppose not."

He leaned forward, bracing his elbows on his knees and focusing on a spot on the floor between his shoes. "When I was a kid—maybe fifteen or sixteen—and my parents went out of town, they'd leave me alone. Jessica would always stay at your house—with you and your dad and your grandparents—but they'd leave me alone. In that crypt of a house." He laughed, but it was a bitter sound. "They thought it was a privilege."

"Brad, you could have stayed with—"

He held up a hand, effectively silencing her. "No, I couldn't. Not after my dad made such a big deal out of letting me stay alone. He thought it was an honor. A sign I was a man. He thought I'd be thrilled to stay at home alone. I thought so, too, at first. But after that first night, I—the house was so empty." Again he laughed, but this time there was at least a hint of humor in the sound. "God, it was bad enough with all four of us there—always so solemn and serious—but alone? When the house was empty? It was..."

He never finished the sentence, but in her mind she finished it for him.

Chilling.

It's what she would have thought. His description of the house as a crypt was dead-on. The Sumner family home—like his parents—had been cold, unwelcoming and sparse. An icy still life of a home, of a family.

She could only imagine how desolate that house would seem to a fifteen-year-old boy left all alone.

"Jess and I always figured you had wild parties at the house when your parents went out of town," she mused.

"Only once." He glanced up at her, a lopsided grin transforming his face with boyish mischief. "My father always ordered me not to have parties. So when I was seventeen, I had one. I figured if I broke his confidence in me, they would stop leaving me by myself. I invited over the entire football team and raided the liquor cabinet."

"Did it work? Was your father furious?"

"No. I think he was actually proud of me. He kept slapping me on the back and saying things like 'Boys will be boys.' Then he got me a summer job at his office and docked my pay to cover the damages."

"Ouch."

"Then a couple of months later, they went to Lake Tahoe for the weekend and left me alone again. It was my eighteenth birthday."

"And you spent it alone," she surmised.

"Not completely. When I dropped Jess off at your house, I hung around until your grandma took the hint and invited me to stay for dinner. It was one of your grandfather's strange creations. Something with tofu and peanuts."

"His vegetarian Pad Thai. Awful stuff."

"But your grandma had made an apple pie for dessert. Honest-to-God, homemade apple pie, fresh out of the oven." He shook his head with a chuckle. "I'd never tasted anything like it."

"That was early in the fall. When the apples where fresh."

She remembered maybe a half-dozen times he'd eaten dinner at her house, but the events blurred together in a collage of nervous excitement. She'd been blinded by his presence and had never noticed that one of those evenings had been his birthday or that he'd ever been anything but thrilled to be dropping his kid sister off for the weekend.

"A couple weeks later, when I filled out the goal chart in Mrs. Winslow's class, I knew what I wanted. I wanted a family. Not like the family I had, but like yours. Loud and busy. With lots of pets and people coming and going and bad food and apple pie."

Her heart—already so weakened by his proximity—turned over. She crossed to the sofa then sat beside him. She touched his arm, hoping to comfort him, though her instincts told her to pull his head to her shoulder and rock him gently back and forth, the way she would a troubled child. Or any deeply wounded soul, for that matter.

Despite his intense vulnerability, his arm felt warm beneath her fingers. And strong. As vibrant as his personality, unweakened by his sorrow.

At her touch, he turned his head to look at her. He was so close. She could see every fleck of silver in his blue eyes. His shoulder brushed against hers, so she could feel his chest move with every exhalation. The warmth of his skin seeped through his shirt and the equally thin fabric of her blouse.

His lips twisted into a wry smile. "I know what you're going to say."

"You do?" Her words sounded as breathless as she felt. But she was glad someone knew what she going to say, because she didn't have a clue.

He nodded. "You're going to tell me that families like that take a lot of work. That they're not something you just decide you want. They don't just magically appear."

She nodded in return. "That sounds like something I'd say."

He ducked his head. "It seems like every step I take just puts me further away from what I want."

The resignation in his voice tore at her. The strength of her reaction, deep and emotional—like falling in love with him all over again—surprised her. In that instant, she realized how right Lucy had been. Where this man was concerned, she was already a goner.

Doing what would be easiest on her was no longer an option. It no longer mattered how much she struggled to keep him out of her heart. She wasn't fighting a losing battle. She was fighting a battle she'd already lost.

Suddenly all her good intentions crumbled. Why was she pushing him away when she wanted him so desperately? Why was she denying herself the one thing she'd always wanted?

Because she thought she could protect her heart? It

was much too late for that anyway. Why not give in to what they both needed? If she only had him for a couple of weeks, she'd have to make those weeks wonderful.

14

SHE DIDN'T MEAN to kiss him. It just sort of happened. An accident. Like the time in college she'd tripped, fallen partway down a flight of stairs and broken her foot. One minute the world was right-side up and her feet were firmly on the ground, the next she was tumbling, free-falling, helplessly headed for disaster.

One minute she was gently stroking his arm, murmuring something reassuring. The next, he'd twisted to face her and the temptation of having him so close was simply too much to resist. Her mind cut off and she leaned forward to press her lips to his.

Instantly she pulled back, surprised by the warmth of his mouth. But one taste simply wasn't enough. She had to have more.

Leaning forward for another kiss, she pulled her feet up under her, angling closer to him. His lips were warm and soft beneath hers. Pliant. As if he hadn't yet decided whether or not to kiss her back. But he tasted wonderful, spicy and sweet. Like cinnamon sugar.

And she simply couldn't get enough of him.

She felt his arms tense beneath her hands. Then, in one smooth movement, he wrapped one arm around her back and the other beneath her legs and he pulled her onto his lap. Her hip brushed his groin as he deepened the kiss. She nearly groaned when she felt his erection against her leg. His hand clutched her bottom, pulling her against him.

The feel of his mouth on hers, of his hands on her body, went straight to her head. But it wasn't enough. Not nearly enough.

Without breaking contact with his mouth, she twisted, shifting her legs so she straddled his lap. She eased her weight down on him, arching her back as the apex of her legs rubbed against his erection. His hands settled on her hips, pulling her toward him, increasing the pressure against her body. Heat and urgency washed over her in alternating waves.

She buried her hands in his hair, holding his mouth beneath hers, trying desperately to ease the tension building within her. Yet, she couldn't get close enough to him, couldn't feel enough of his body. Her fingers tripped down the buttons on his shirt, but before she loosened any of them, his fingers grasped hers and pulled them away.

"Wait." He sounded as out of breath as she felt. "Are you sure?"

Unsure whether to laugh or scream in frustration, she rotated her hips against him. "Oh, yes."

He squeezed his eyes closed and a pained expression flashed across his face. She lowered her mouth to his, infusing the kiss with years of pent-up longing. Last night had happened so quickly. Tonight she wanted to take her time. To explore his body and learn all his secrets. But passion hit her quickly, urging her on.

Her fingers worked frantically on his buttons, twisting and shoving aside fabric as she went. When she finally felt his naked skin beneath her hands, her fingers tightened, relishing the heat of him and the hardened muscles beneath.

He broke free of her lips to trail kisses down her neck. When he found the sensitive spot just below her ear, she groaned aloud, arching to give him access to all of her throat. His fingers tore at the buttons of her shirt, but their fumbling only frustrated her. She ached to feel his hands on her bare flesh and he simply wasn't moving fast enough.

She shoved his hands aside and yanked the partially unbuttoned shirt over her head, tossing it carelessly behind her. He pulled back far enough to look at her. The stark longing in his expression sent shivers of pleasure through her.

With a single fingertip, he traced an uneven line down her throat to the crest of one of her breasts. He slipped his finger beneath the fabric of her bra, brushing her hardened nipple with his knuckle.

"So beautiful," he murmured. He lowered his mouth to her nipple, stopping just shy of pulling the aching flesh into his mouth. He raised his eyes to hers. "I want to please you," he stated simply.

The heat of his breath warmed her through the silken fabric. Feeling suddenly bolder than she'd ever felt with a man, she reached behind her and, with a flick of her fingers, unhooked her bra. She quickly shucked the scrap of fabric then cupped her breasts in her hands, offering them to him. "Then stop talking," she said gently.

He needed no further encouragement. With his hands and his mouth he laved attention on her body. He suckled and nipped. Nibbled as if to devour her. As if to consume not only her flesh, but her very soul.

But even this wasn't enough. Not for her. As if he could read her thoughts, he sensed her impatience. Holding her body close to his, he stood. Automatically she wrapped her legs around him, locking her ankles behind his back. Still kissing her, he took the few steps down the hall that led to both of their bedrooms.

She pulled her mouth from his long enough to gasp out an order. "My room. It's closer."

He stumbled into her room, plowing right into the bed, where he fell, rolling onto his back so she rested on top. They landed on the bed, a mass of arms, legs and laughter. She wiggled her legs out from under him as they kissed. Her body pulsated with the sheer joy of being so wanted by him.

She rolled away from him long enough to yank off all of her remaining clothes except for her pink cotton bikini panties. Then she scrambled to the edge of the bed, tugged open the drawer of her nightstand and dug frantically through the contents. Finally she pulled out an unopened box of condoms and held it up victoriously.

"Aha! I knew they were in there. They were a gift from Lucy, who's become rabid about safe..." Her words trailed off when she noticed how still and silent he'd become. He lay beside her, shirt unbuttoned and shoes off, neatly pressed Dockers still on. The delicious contrast between the raw masculinity of his bare chest and his serious-businessman pants might have been enough to distract her if she hadn't seen the earnest expression on his face.

The box of condoms fell to the bed, unnoticed. "Brad?" He said nothing but continued to study her. Self-consciously she ran a hand down to the elastic edge of her panties. She shrugged dismissively. "Not very sexy, I guess."

His brow furrowed, then he shook his head and reached for her. He pulled her down beside him, propping his weight on his elbow beside her shoulder. "No, they're perfect." With an almost reverent touch, he brushed the hair from her forehead. "You're perfect. But I—" Again he frowned, seemingly unwilling to meet her eyes.

She said nothing, but waited for him to finish his thought.

"Other than last night, I haven't...been with a woman since Ginger."

The admission seemed hard for him, pulled from deep within his gut. In her relief, she almost laughed at the obviousness of his statement. Instead, she ran her fingers down the length of his jaw and made an admission of her own. "I hadn't been with a man since Mike, either."

Hoping to regain their earlier playfulness, she ran her foot up his leg and toyed with the back of his knee. She reached behind her for the cardboard box and handed it to him. "Now, be a good boy and finish what you started."

He quirked an eyebrow. "Or?"

She nearly sighed in relief—disaster had been averted. "Or I may have to give you detention."

His lips twisted into a sexy grin. "Oh, really? I certainly don't want that."

"I should think not."

Reaching between them, she unbuckled his belt. Her fingers fumbled with the closure of his pants, too eager to maintain the mischievous banter for long. Slipping her hands under his waistband, she felt his abdomen tighten at her touch. His reaction sent a shiver of heat through her belly.

She ran her palms under his pants and down his buttocks. Silk boxers. Oh, boy.

Exhaling slowly, she helped him pull his pants the rest of the way off. She fondled him through his boxers, luxuriating in the feel of his rigid length beneath the silk.

But touching him wasn't enough. She wanted more. She wanted all of him. His gasp told her he wanted the same. They moved quickly, suddenly frantic to join their bodies, tossing aside clothes and groping for the condom. Not nearly soon enough, he thrust inside her.

It was as if her whole body breathed a sigh of relief. As if her whole existence had been leading up to this one moment. This one perfect union of anticipation, completion and emotion.

She moved against him, meeting his every thrust, moaning his name and crying in relief as her body spasmed around him. A second later, the muscles of his back tightened beneath her fingers as he reached his own release.

Then he rolled onto his back, pulling her to his side. As she lay in his arms, murmuring his name against his still-heaving chest, she realized how completely ridiculous her plan had been to banish Brad from her fantasies.

Twice now, they'd had sex, but it wasn't bad sex. In some ways, it was exactly what she'd wanted. Clumsy and impatient. But also wonderful, messy and spontaneous. But not at all bad.

She cuddled closer to his chest, trying to fight off the feeling that she'd made a very bad mistake. Brad had not disappointed her in bed, but she felt certain that before this was over, he would disappoint her heart.

BRAD NEVER SLEPT LATE. In fact, he hadn't slept past nine in the morning since he'd gotten drunk his freshman year of college, slept till noon the next day and missed his economics exam.

So he was more than a little surprised to roll over, crack open his eyes and see a tepid ray of late-morning sun creeping through a gap in Mattie's curtains. He blinked sleepily before rubbing the grit from his eyes with the back of his hand.

He knew without looking that Mattie no longer lay beside him in bed. She'd slept curled against him for most of the night, and he missed the warmth of having her near. Missed waking up beside her and making slow, sleepy love to her first thing in the morning.

But the solitude did give him a chance to think.

All this time, he'd been saying he didn't want an-other wife. Mattie hadn't believed him. Well, it turned out, she was right. He did want another wife. He wanted her.

Why hadn't he seen it before?

All his life, he'd wanted a family like the one she'd grown up in. If he married her, he'd have it.

Every night he could make love to her. Every morn-ing he could wake up with her in his bed. Well, her and Avenue.

Mattie had insisted on letting Avenue in late last night, after they made love. The dog had first slept on the floor beside the bed and then moved to the foot of the bed in the night.

He'd grumbled about Avenue's invasion, until Mat-tie had snuggled against him to make room for the dog. As he lay there in the night, both Mattie and Av-enue in bed with him, for the first time in his adult life, he felt completely content. As if the life he'd always wanted was within his grasp. His contentment had nothing to do with that stupid list of life goals he'd written at eighteen or whether or not he'd achieved them, but everything to do with the woman lying be-side him.

The woman who seemed to know him better than he knew himself. She'd been right about so many things. First off, mindlessly pursuing his goals had not made him happy. Secondly, he had named Maddie after her—subconsciously at least—because he'd wanted that connection to his past. To her.

And if she was right about that, he began to wonder, what else might she be right about? Ginger, maybe? The fact that the failings in their relationship weren't his fault alone?

If he wasn't responsible for Ginger's unhappiness in their marriage, then there was nothing keeping him from marrying Mattie. Except the fact that she lived here and he lived in San Francisco. A relatively minor detail, really.

Especially when he considered how much she'd given up for others. She didn't love quilting or the quilt shop. She'd taken over the shop only to satisfy her grandmother.

If they got married, he could give her everything she'd ever wanted. She could sell the quilt shop, move back to San Francisco with him and go back to teaching. Maybe he'd even take her to Brazil for their honeymoon.

HE WAS STILL PLANNING out his proposal when he heard the muffled noise of someone moving around the house, a door open and close. The scuffle of paws crossing tile. The distant off-key humming of some unrecognizable pop song. All accompanied by the faint scent of cinnamon.

He sat up, but before he could even swing his legs over the side of the bed, the bedroom door creaked open and she peaked around through the gap. Though he saw only a sliver of her face—a tousled lock of brown hair, a glint of mischief in a moss-green eye, and a rosy cheek—he could tell she was up to something.

"You're up," she said, toeing open the door.

With a shoulder propped against the doorjamb and a hand held behind her back, she studied him. A slow, sexy smile tugged at her lips. "Good morning."

"Good morning, yourself." The smile and the glint in her eye packed a brutal punch and he wanted nothing more than to pull her back onto the bed and spend the rest of the morning—hell, the rest of the day—making love to her. If the gleam in her eye was any indication, she wouldn't argue.

To coax her into the room, he asked, "What's that you've got behind your back?"

Her smile broadened. "I made you breakfast." Without showing her hand, she sauntered into the room.

She wore a white T-shirt and yellow shorts. It was a simple girlish outfit that wouldn't have looked sexy on any woman but her.

But on her... Oh, man. The flared legs of the shorts emphasized the sway of her hips as she walked. The cropped length displayed slender, tanned legs. The fabric of her T-shirt was just thin enough to reveal she wasn't wearing a bra beneath it.

That first day, when he'd seen her wearing only a bath towel, he'd thought he'd never wanted a woman more. Maybe he'd been right. But it was nothing compared to the way he craved her now. Hell, he never would have imagined he could want this badly a woman he'd spent the entire previous night making love to.

When she sat primly on the edge of the bed beside him, it was all he could do not to pull her right into his arms. Instead, he leaned back against the pillows and asked, "Breakfast, huh?"

She bit down on her lip, doing a very poor job of suppressing her smile. "You wanna guess what it is?"

Unable to resist the temptation of touching her, he trailed his hand up her leg to the hem of her shorts. Her skin was warm and resilient. Touching her proved to be a mistake, because he didn't want to stop. "I'm hoping it's something that can wait."

With her free hand, she swatted his away. "Behave or I won't share with you."

"Share what?"

"This." She pulled her hand from behind her back. The dinner plate she held bore a fat slice of pie complete with a scoop of vanilla ice cream.

"Pie."

"Not just pie. Fresh, homemade apple pie." With the fork, she sliced off the tip of the pie and dabbed a bit of ice cream. "I woke up early. You were still dead to the world, so I drove out to Apple Hill." She extended the fork to him. "Wanna taste?"

He leaned forward and parted his lips. She slipped the bit of pie neatly into his mouth. The crust flaked against his tongue. His taste buds registered the sweet filling, the bite of cinnamon and the chill of the ice cream, but he could barely swallow past the lump in his throat.

She seemed not to notice his lack of response but kept talking, forking off another chunk of pie.

"I used to love the fall because of the pies Grandma would make." She extended the fork to him again, and again he opened his mouth to receive it. "I haven't made one in years." She popped a bite in her mouth, rambling as she chewed. "It's ridiculous. Having fresh apples so close and not making better use of them. I should—"

He reached for her hand, stopped her just short of plopping another bite into his mouth. "Mattie, no one's ever—"

She met his gaze, her eyes clear and shining with honesty. As if she knew exactly what he'd been about to say—when he didn't even know himself—she nodded, suddenly serious. "I know."

And he sensed she did. Staring into her eyes, he couldn't shake the feeling that no one would ever understand him the way she did, right now. As if, in this single perfect moment, the emotional bond between them was as strong as the physical one had been the night before.

An instant later, the moment was gone. She playfully nudged the bite of pie in his direction. A dollop of melting ice cream dropped from the fork onto his arm.

"Oops," she cooed. She diverted the pie to her own mouth, then set the plate on the bed. Crawling onto his lap, she grasped his hand, extending his arm until the drop of cream was within reach of her lips. Her eyes wide with mock innocence, she mused, "I guess eating in bed can be messy."

"Oh, you think that was messy?" He reached for the plate.

Before he could break off a chunk of pie, she pulled her shirt off with a shrug and tossed it aside. The bite he offered her never made it to her mouth. He sucked pie filling from her chin, nibbled flakes of crust off her breast and lapped a stream of melted ice cream across her belly.

They ate the rest of the pie the same way. Feeding each other sloppy forkfuls of pie, missing their mouths more often than not, sampling each other's bodies until the pie was gone, their skin was sticky and their breath came in short bursts.

He rolled her onto her back, desperate to be inside her, amazed that he'd waited as long as he had. A lifetime, it seemed.

As he eased himself into her welcoming heat, he kissed her. She tasted of apple pie, cinnamon and vanilla. Like sin and salvation rolled into one. Like everything he'd ever wanted but never knew how to ask for.

But now he knew.

15

HE'D NEVER MET a business he couldn't fix. Sure, some places had more problems than others did. That was just the way of the world. The good news was, for him at least, solving A Stitch in Time's problems was going to be relatively easy. And brief.

That was the good news. The bad news was, when Mattie heard the changes he was suggesting, she wouldn't like them. But she was a businesswoman. Surely she would be able to distance herself emotionally from the problems with the shop.

And yet, as he settled into the chair facing her desk, he hesitated a moment. He realized now that he wanted to be able to fix her problems. Not because he owed it to her—though he did—but because he wanted to be the one who rescued her. He wanted her to once again look at him and see her hero. Maybe if he saved her business, she would.

The tiny room, dimly lit by a single overhead fixture, radiated with the warmth of Mattie's personality. The ancient wood desk, the kitschy, Depression-era wall clock, and the inviting armchair she'd gestured him into all screamed of waste and frivolity. Comfortable excess.

He'd seen it a dozen times before. Small, family-run

businesses that devoted countless resources to creating a "friendly" environment. What a waste.

"So, what do you think of my place?" As she spoke, her fingers toyed with the neckline of her bright-yellow T-shirt. Whether she meant to or not—and he suspected not—she drew his attention to the delicate hollow of her throat.

He moved his attention away from her, pretending to read from the lined paper on which he'd taken notes. "It's obvious you've invested a lot of time and energy into making this store—" he decided not to sugarcoat the facts "—comfortable."

"That's exactly what I was trying to do." Unfortunately, she took the criticism as a compliment. Her eyes lit up as she spoke. "When I was a child—when my grandma owned the shop—it was my special place. Sort of my retreat from the rest of the world. I want my customers to feel that way, too."

The conviction behind her words only reminded him that Mattie never did anything half-heartedly. Her devotion to the store was rooted in the same passion she brought to everything in her life. Her friends, her family, their lovemaking.

He remembered how she'd looked at him last night, through half-closed eyes clouded with passion. The memory made him shift in his chair and adjust his leather portfolio across his lap.

Damn. This was going to be harder than he thought. In more ways than one.

But lying to her wouldn't help her. Only honesty would do that. And as much as he wanted to keep her in his bed, he wasn't willing to sacrifice her store to do it. And if he was lucky he wouldn't have to. "Don't worry. I've developed a three-point plan to fix it."

"Fix it?" Her eyes met his full on and her emotions were telecast in her eyes. Confusion, doubt, then anger all warred within her. "Fix it?" she asked again.

"Yes, fix it. Your store space is larger than you need. You have too much capital invested in inventory. And your staff is poorly trained or incompetent."

Mattie shot to her feet, fury delineated on every line of her face. "What?"

Maybe he should have phrased that differently, taken into account the irrational attachment women sometimes placed on things. He was used to dealing with men and women who'd been mired in corporate culture long enough to overcome whatever sentimentality they might have.

This was, after all, her store. And her grandmother's store. Hoping to calm her, he deliberately slowed his speech. "Now, Mattie—"

"Oh, don't you dare 'now Mattie' me." She planted her palms firmly on the desk and leaned forward. The neck of her T-shirt gaped, granting him a glimpse of her breasts and of the white lace cupping them. But when she spoke, her voice was hard enough to command his attention. "I want to know exactly what you meant when you said my staff was incompetent."

"Let me back up and take you step-by-step through my three-point plan."

Her lips thinned to an almost invisible line and—he winced—it looked like she'd developed a tick in her right eye. Nevertheless, she straightened, tugged at the hem of her shirt and lowered herself back into her chair. "Yes. Please do."

The chill of her response washed across the desk like a wave of arctic seawater. For once, he regretted having to do his job. "First, your store is too comfortable."

She leaned forward, hands once again braced on the edge of her desk. "It's supposed to be comfortable."

"Stopping me every sentence isn't the most efficient way to go through this."

She eyed him for a second before leaning back in her chair and crossing her arms over her chest. He tried not to notice the wonderful things the posture did for her breasts, focusing instead on her body language. From aggressive to defensive. Not much progress.

"Maybe it would be better if I wrote this up in a report. Then you could go over it at your own pace when you're feeling less emotional."

"Less emotional? What's that supposed to mean?"

"You've already closed yourself to my suggestions. I can read it in your body language. If I'm going to help you, you'll have to calm down."

"How exactly am I supposed to do that? You're attacking something I've devoted years of my life to."

"I'm criticizing it. Not attacking." He sighed, not sure what to say to make her listen. "If this store was a person, a person who had cancer, you'd want to know where the cancer was. That way, you could operate, eliminate the cancer and in doing so, save the healthy organs."

"I guess."

"That's all I'm doing here. I'm looking for the cancer."

"Fine. Just be aware that I won't let you operate unless I agree with your prognosis." Slowly, almost reluctantly, she uncrossed her arms. She rested one hand on the arm of her chair and picked up a pencil from the desk with the other. "Why don't you tell me about this three-point plan of yours."

Okay, fixing Mattie's store, take two.

He exhaled slowly. "First your store is too comfortable." The muscles in her jawline tightened, but she said nothing. Since he could tell she wanted to, he felt compelled to explain. "The more comfortable people feel, the more likely they are to leave without buying anything."

"Those two things aren't related at all."

"They are. Customers who feel comfortable, who feel at home, don't feel like they have to spend money."

"Customers who feel comfortable come back."

"Which is irrelevant if they never spend money."

"They do spend money."

"Not today they didn't. While I was here, four women came in, looked around, consulted with your sales associates and still didn't buy anything."

"They aren't sales associates. They're quilting experts. They are supposed to be consulted."

"They missed an opportunity to make a sale. A trained salesperson would have sold those customers something. They lost you money today. There's a woman out there right now who brought in a bag of her own fabric and her own supplies. She's using your space—space you're paying rent for—she's wasting the time of your 'quilting experts'—whose salaries you pay—and she's probably not going to spend a dime."

"That woman is most likely a repeat customer. She probably bought most of that fabric and most of those supplies here. There are tons of women who do this all the time. They come in, they look around, they ask a few a questions. Maybe they buy something, maybe they don't. But they come in once or twice a week. Sometimes just to see the new inventory. I want them to come. I want them to feel comfortable."

Apprehension began to creep through his belly. She'd shot down point one of his three-point plan. Shot it right out the sky. Customer comfort leads to customer loyalty. It was a concept deserving further consideration.

He moved on to the next point. "Inventory. That's another problem."

"My inventory? I've got the biggest selection in Northern California. What's wrong with my inventory?"

"You've got the biggest selection in Northern California. That's your problem. You've got too much capital invested in your inventory."

"Too much capital? That's crazy."

"You carry over thirty fabrics that are predominantly red. I counted."

"Oh, I'm sure you did. I have thirty-three to be exact and two more coming in tomorrow's shipment. What's your point?"

"That no store needs to carry over fifty green fabrics."

"The human eye distinguishes more shades of green than any other color."

"I didn't know that." Brad clenched his jaw, then forced himself to relax. This wasn't going well and he didn't like it.

"Apparently there's a lot you don't know." She rose from her chair, paced to the far wall, then shot him a look over her shoulder. "I believe next you were going to insult my employees."

"Maybe this isn't a good time." He stood and, when he took a step toward her, she turned away, feigning interest in her books. "I'll come ba—"

Her head jerked around, and he was surprised to see she'd banked the anger in her eyes. "You'll come back when? When I'm more rational? When I can sit here and coolly listen to you dissect and denigrate the only part of my life I'm proud of? When I can remain calm while you tear down the things my grandmother worked for her entire adult life?"

"I'm sorry."

"No." She sighed. "I'm sorry. I asked for your help—I insisted you give it—but I'm not making this very easy on you." She crossed to stand in front of him, half sitting on the edge of her desk. "Maybe it would help if I explained about the three of them."

He doubted it; nevertheless, he nodded so she'd continue. Not so much because he thought that whatever she was going to say would change his mind about her employees, but more because he wanted the insight into her.

"I can imagine how they look to you. Lucy is young and pregnant and—well, you've met her—I'm not going to pretend she's an intellectual giant. Yes, I hired her only because I felt sorry for her. But she's smarter than she looks and she has an amazing eye for color and she makes more sales than any of the rest of us. Probably because people feel sorry for her."

He nodded, this time because he could see her point. While showing him around the store, Lucy had seemed so vulnerable, so pitiful, he'd been tempted to buy something from her himself.

"As for Abigail and Edith," Mattie continued. "They've worked here longer than I have. Yes, they're old, but together they have more quilting experience than anyone else in the central valley. Sure, I know what you're going to say. Abigail's eyesight isn't what it used to be and Edith's hands shake so that sometimes her stitches—" Mattie broke off, her gaze straying up to the far corner of the room, her eyes a little too wide, a little too bright. "Her stitches are a little crooked. I know that. But there was a time when she could stitch a quilt so lovely it'd make you cry."

She levered herself away from the desk and straightened her shoulders. "Don't you dare tell me their past experience counts for nothing. I know how they must seem to you. Lucy—pregnant at nineteen—seems stupid, and Edith and Abigail seem frail, worthless, but they *are* valuable. I'm not going to go out there and tell any of those women that they're not needed. The store needs them. I need them.''

''You've mistaken my meaning. I didn't say your employees aren't valuable.''

''Excuse me, but that's exactly what you said.''

''I understand you're fond of them, but this is business. You may have to choose. If you're not taking in enough money to pay your bills, you have to cut your expenses or you'll go out of business.''

''Then I'll go out of business.''

''You're not being logical.''

''Maybe not, but if I have to choose between the shop and the people, then I choose the people.''

''You'd sacrifice your grandmother's shop for them?''

''Yes, I would. It's what she would do.''

Brad shook his head, not quite sure what to make of her. His work, his company, meant everything to him. There wasn't anyone—not anyone in the world—he'd sacrifice his company to protect. And, he realized with a sharp pang, there was no one who'd make that kind of sacrifice for him.

''Mattie, I'm trying to understand, but letting even one employee go could make the difference.''

''No,'' she snapped. ''I'm not letting anyone go and that's final.''

''But—''

''If one person's salary is so important,'' her voice rose sharply, ''then I'll give up mine.''

''And live on what? I've seen your books—you don't

take home enough to live on as it is. Your salary wouldn't pay for half of one of theirs."

"Then I'll get another job."

"And work in the evenings just so you can pay them?"

She paced to the door then spun back around. "Yes, if I have to."

"That's not logical. Reducing the staff may be the only long-term solution."

"Then I don't need a long-term solution. I need a miracle."

And with that, she was gone. Out the door and maybe—dear God, he hoped not—out of his life.

He sank to the chair, propped his elbows on his knees and rubbed his forehead.

Damn. He'd blown it. Boy, had he blown it.

He'd never even gotten to the part where he suggested selling the store and moving to San Francisco with him. Somehow, he didn't think she'd like that idea any better.

The trouble was he couldn't think of anything he could have done differently. He'd given her good advice. Sure, maybe he hadn't fully grasped all the intricacies of the quilting business. He hadn't been informed about the peculiar qualities of quilting customers. But if he'd been off base about his first two suggestions, then that only made his third suggestion more valid.

Something had to give. He just hoped it wasn't Mattie. As far as he could tell, she'd given enough already.

"You made her cry."

Brad looked up to see Lucy standing in the doorway to the office, flanked on either side by Edith and Abigail. Collectively they looked ready to lynch him. The image of being hung by a quilted noose flashed through his mind. He laughed grimly at the visual.

They didn't see the humor he did. As one, they stepped into the room, fists propped on hips, eyes narrowed in defensive anger.

He held up his hands in surrender. "Wait. I didn't mean to. She's just upset about the—" He racked his brain for a suitable lie, but couldn't construct one. "About the books. She's worried about the shop."

Infinitesimally the three women relaxed.

"Well, hang it all," Edith said. "We know that. But we don't know what to do to help."

"No, we don't," added Lucy. "We offered to take pay cuts, but she wouldn't listen."

"Oh, dear," Abigail murmured. "We had hoped things were picking up. After all, a strong woman knows her own mind and her own limits."

Brad nodded as if he understood. He'd spent most of the morning with Abigail but had only gotten about half of what she said. "I'm afraid Mattie's about reached hers."

"Humph," Edith stepped forward to stand in front of the other two women. "What can we do to help?"

Brad assessed the women standing before him. He considered sharing his three-point plan with them but dismissed the idea. If their protective reaction so far was any indication, they'd be fighting each other for the right to be fired. Mattie would never forgive him if he accidentally fired all three of her employees.

He shook his head. "I'm not sure there's anything we can do."

"Nonsense," Edith insisted. "You're the brilliant businessman. Come up with a solution."

Abigail placed her hand on Edith's arm. "Edith dear, the willow that bends survives the storm."

Edith shrugged off the hand. "Poppycock. I'm not a willow and neither is Mattie. There has to be something we can do."

Lucy, less philosophical, stamped her foot. "It's just not fair. I don't see why she has to pay off her stupid ex's debt. It's not like—"

Abigail nudged Lucy. Edith interrupted her, "Well, Mr. Sumners, let us know if we can be of service."

"What debt?"

"All that debt from her—"

This time, both of the old women nudged Lucy so hard she swayed back and forth between them. "Ow. That hurts. Stop poking me."

"What debt?" he asked again.

Lucy opened her mouth then snapped it closed.

Edith squared off her shoulders. "I'm sure Mattie's given you all the information she thinks you need."

Brad shot out of his chair, knocking it back several inches in the process. "What debt?" He pinned Lucy with his gaze, sensing she was the weakest link in this chain.

However, Lucy didn't even flinch. It was Abigail

who elbowed Edith aside and stepped forward. "Mike's debt."

Edith gasped, spinning around to face the other woman. "Abigail, how—"

Abigail shook her head. "Now Edith, he's just here to help. He can't help Mattie or the store if he doesn't have all the information."

Edith's brow knit and she crossed her arms over her chest and grunted suspiciously.

Tapping his fingers against the side of his thigh, he said—for what he hoped was the last time, "What about Mike's debt?"

Abigail twisted her fingers together and stepped farther into the room. "Oh, dear, this is complicated. Perhaps you should sit back down." Crossing to the other side of Mattie's desk, Abigail pointed to the chair Brad had recently abandoned.

With surprising dexterity, Abigail angled the computer monitor in his direction and jiggled the mouse to deactivate the screen saver. With a few arthritic clicks of the mouse, she pulled up an overview of the store's finances.

"Here it is." Abigail pointed to a column labeled General Operating Expenses. "For a long time we didn't realize what it meant. But she finally admitted it."

"Admitted what?"

"She's paying back Mike's loan. He took out a loan against the store. Lucy noticed it a couple months ago."

Lucy stepped forward now. "Yeah. In the file, she has it labeled General Operating Expenses. But what does that mean? I didn't know, so I asked. It wasn't the rent or the electricity bill or the suppliers. It wasn't any of the things that seemed like they'd be general operating expenses because they all have their own columns."

Brad angled his head to reassess the girl. Smarter than she looked? Apparently. She'd noticed something he'd overlooked completely.

"That's when we noticed it was the same amount every month and that it went to the bank," Abigail added.

Brad propped his elbows on the desk as he leaned forward to study the screen. "So basically, if it wasn't for the loan she has to pay off, the store would be in the black."

"We'd be making plenty of money, if that's what you mean," Edith said.

"It's not fair that she has to pay back that jerk's debt," Lucy rubbed her belly nervously. "Surely, there's something you can do to help, Mr. Sumners."

Once again, he rubbed his hand across his forehead. The beginnings of one hell of a tension headache crawled up his neck. "I'm not sure there is."

Lucy frowned. "Couldn't you talk to the bank? Explain about Mike. It's his fault. He's the one who should have to pay it back."

"I don't think it works that way."

"But there's got to be something you can do. There just has to be."

He turned back to the women, relieved at least that they no longer looked ready to start quilting his noose.

"How much does she owe?" All three frowned. "What kind of percentage rate is she getting?" The frowns deepened. "What bank is the loan from?"

Finally, he got a response.

"Hamilton Trust." Lucy leaned over Abigail to thumb through the Rolodex. She found the card she wanted, yanked it from its position and handed it to him. "It's a local company. They specialize in home and small business loans."

Brad smiled at her as he took the card. Score another point for Lucy. "I'll see what I can do. But first I have to talk to Mattie."

And he had to come up with a miracle.

16

"TELL ME ABOUT MIKE."

Mattie stilled, a bag of chocolate chips poised above the mixing bowl. Her hand clenched on the package and a few chips tumbled in. Deliberately she shook half the chips into the bowl before asking, "What do you want to know?"

She heard the tapping of Brad's shoes as he crossed the tile floor to stand beside her. In her peripheral vision, she saw him lean against the counter and cross his arms over his chest. "Tell me about the money."

She squeezed her eyes shut. When she opened them, she dumped the rest of the bag in the bowl—the day she was having definitely called for double chocolate chips. Then she flipped the mixer on and waited for the consolation only raw cookie dough could provide.

She turned to face him. "They told you about the loan," she surmised. He nodded. "They shouldn't have said anything."

"I pressured them."

She almost laughed at that. "Right. You're the last person I'd expect to hear defending them."

"They only wanted to help."

"I know." She flipped the mixer off, extracted the bowl of cookie dough and retrieved a soupspoon from the drawer. She scraped a mound of dough onto the spoon then held it out to him. After all, she didn't want to be rude.

He accepted the spoon but held it out in front of himself. He turned the spoon this way and that, studying it from all angles. If she'd handed him a freshly skinned pig's snout he couldn't have looked more perplexed.

"Are there raw eggs in this?" he asked as she loaded her own spoon.

"Better not to think about it."

He frowned then held the utensil farther away from his body, as if the bacteria could propel themselves through the air.

She took pity on him. "Don't worry. I use pasteurized eggs."

"About Mike—" he began.

She didn't give him a chance to finish. "I didn't tell you about the loan because I didn't want you to know how stupid I'd been." She nibbled at the edges of her spoon of cookie dough, finding just enough fortification to continue. "Mike had this way about him. He could convince anyone of anything. He could explain things that didn't really make sense so that it seemed like they did."

"What does that have to do with the loan?"

Brad, apparently suddenly willing to try the cookie dough, raised the spoon to his lips and ran his tongue across the lump of dough.

Man, Brad could do things for cookie dough that the Pillsbury Doughboy could never imagine. Mattie closed her eyes and bit down on her spoon.

"When we got married, Mike worked for this small computer company. The pay sucked, but they gave him tons of stock options. He swore it was going to be the next Yahoo. As soon as the company went public, we'd be rich.

"It wasn't bad at first. We pretty much lived on my salary. Money was tight, but I thought we did okay. But then Mike wanted to buy a house. He said it was stupid to throw our money away on rent, but we needed money for the down payment. By then, I'd stopped teaching. I'd inherited the quilt store outright and was running it. That's when we took out the loan against the store. It was a lot of money, but I thought we were getting by."

Mattie grimaced at her spoon. Suddenly even chocolate-chip cookie dough didn't taste good. She tossed the spoon into the sink and covered the mixing bowl with plastic wrap.

Brad tossed his spoon aside also. "But...?" He let the question hang in the air.

"But then I found out about his credit card debt. It wasn't just one or two. It was tens of thousands of dollars on dozens of credit cards. There was no way we could have ever paid them back. That's when I knew it was over." Her memories flashed back to those last horrible weeks of her marriage.

She let out a nervous laugh. "It's odd. Everyone thought I left him because of the other women. But that wasn't it. The other women weren't really that bad. A one-night stand every two or three years—I know it sounds weak, but I could've overlooked that indefinitely."

Besides, there was no room in her heart to criticize him. If he gave his body to other women, how could she complain? She'd long ago given her heart to another man.

She shrugged. "I wasn't happy about it, but I always believed marriage was forever. And he was always sorry afterward. So apologetic.

"But the money." She felt her eyes tearing up against her will, so she shook her head, hoping for some of that emotional distance Brad said she needed. "I couldn't stand the debt. I couldn't live like that. I thought about it, worried about it, all the time." She laughed again, a bitter, sad laugh. "All I wanted was to not have to worry about money ever again. And I was stupid enough to think divorcing him would make a difference. It didn't. California is a community property state. So we split the property and the debt. He took his half and immediately declared bankruptcy."

Brad hooked his knuckle under her chin and nudged her face up. "But you didn't."

"No. If I declared bankruptcy, I'd lose the store."

"You didn't even consider it, did you?"

Her head jerked up in surprise. "Of course not. That store is everything to me."

"No." He slowly shook his head. "That was everything to your grandmother. It's everything to Edith and Abigail and Lucy. Not to you."

"What do you mean? I love—"

"No, you don't. You love your employees, but you

don't love the store. You don't love quilting. I've watched you. When they start talking about patterns and stitches and fabric content, your eyes glaze over. You don't even quilt."

"I do crazy quilts."

"Because you can't stand doing the real ones. You said it yourself. All those little squares and triangles make you crazy. You gave up something you did love—teaching—so you could run your grandma's store. Don't get me wrong, it's admirable. But if the store's going to fold, why not just let it go? Why not go back to teaching?"

"And just give up without a fight? I'd never do that."

"Because you don't want Edith, Abigail and Lucy to be without jobs? But what about you, Mattie? You deserve to be just as happy as they do."

"You make it sound as if I'm miserable working at the store. I'm not. I may not love quilting, but I love the people. My employees and my customers. And I'm not going to give up on them."

She twisted her head from his hand and sidled away. She poured a glass of water and sipped it, mostly to keep herself busy. She simply couldn't bear his attention any longer.

Finally he broke the silence. "You still should have told me about the loan."

"I didn't tell anyone."

"Your family?" She shook her head. "Jess?" Again she shook her head. "Maybe they could help."

"Maybe. I'd been putting it off. I didn't want anyone

to know how stupid I'd been trusting Mike with our money. We never want the people we love to see us at our worst, do we?''

He shoved his hands in his pockets, ducking his head so she couldn't read his expression. ''No.'' His voice was quiet, his answer almost imperceptible. ''We don't.''

She studied his profile, realizing for the first time how hard telling her about Ginger must have been for him.

There'd been a time in her life when she would have sworn this man had no secrets, no faults, nothing to be ashamed of. Apparently even he was susceptible to those emotions, regardless of whether or not he deserved them. Somehow, she felt better knowing she wasn't the only one who regretted past decisions.

They still stood side by side and she slipped her hand into his and linked their fingers.

''I could loan you money,'' he said unexpectedly.

She looked at him. ''I wouldn't let you even if I thought you had that kind of money lying around.''

''I don't, but I could sell stock, cash in some investments.''

She studied him from under her lashes, tempted to let him solve her problems, wanting to pretend—if only for a moment—that he could be her white knight. Then she blinked and reality returned. ''And what of your 'millionaire by twenty-eight' goal? How would cashing in lucrative investments to help out a buddy affect your net worth? I doubt small-town quilt stores are renowned as sound investments.''

He didn't meet her eyes. "Sound enough."

"Thanks for the offer, but no. Don't worry about us. I'll think of something." Feeling inexplicably light-hearted, she grinned. "Besides I hear Cutie Pies is hiring."

He smiled back. "Don't start taking people's orders just yet. I still might be able to pull off that miracle."

WHEN SHE WOKE UP to an empty bed the next morning, she wasn't surprised. Brad rose early every morning—except for the morning she'd made him apple pie—to do sit-ups and other torturous exercises. Given how much she'd appreciated those stomach muscles last night, she could hardly complain now.

She stretched and yawned, smiling as she remembered the previous night. When they'd made love the night before, he'd been not just passionate, but surprisingly tender. And today was his birthday. She'd have to do something special for him.

Mattie rolled over, burying her nose in the pillow where he'd slept. The pillowcase still held his scent. It smelled like him and—she grinned as she recognized the scent—her bath gel.

Only when she started to climb out of bed did she see him, sitting in her bedroom's only chair, half-hidden by the early-morning gloom. He sat, elbows on his knees, fingers templed, staring at her.

And that's when she knew something was wrong. The relaxed, sexy Brad of last night was gone. She'd been left with the serious intense, businessy Brad.

As much as this intense Brad appealed to her, she

would have preferred to spend her remaining time with the Brad she'd made love to last night. And she knew without even asking that whatever this Brad had to say, she didn't want to hear it.

"I've been thinking." He stood and crossed to the bed. She scooted aside so he'd have room to sit, but he just stood there, hands on his hips, his shirt long gone, his jeans from last night low on his hips.

She smiled limply, praying his next words would be something inconsequential like "Maybe I should get a cat," or "Martin Scorsese is the best director of his generation."

Instead, he said, "This has worked out well. There's no reason we shouldn't consider something more permanent."

Dread knotted in the pit of her stomach. She wiggled into a sitting position, shying away from him as she did so. If she could've bolted from the room, she would have.

"You were right, you know. I do want to be married," he admitted. "You need money. I need a wife. We each are uniquely qualified to meet the other's needs."

"Don't." She squeezed her eyes closed, shaking her head. "Please don't do this."

When she opened her eyes, it was to find him looking at her blankly, as if he couldn't understand her words.

She said nothing, unsure of what to say. He continued. "Mattie, I'm asking you to marry me."

She thought she'd braced herself for those words,

but still they ripped through her. Again she simply shook her head. "Don't."

He either didn't hear her objections or didn't care about them. "You said yourself you never wanted to worry about money again. Marriage to me would ensure that. You'd be financially secure."

Okay, that was it. She couldn't sit here listening to him calmly discuss their relationship as if it were a business deal. She climbed from the bed, pulling the top sheet with her and wrapping it around her body as she walked.

He followed her from the bedroom to the kitchen. "You do still want children, don't you? You did when you were young."

She spun on her heel and stopped him short, her anguish now completely replaced with anger. "Brad, don't."

He blinked in surprise. "Don't what?"

"Just don't, okay? Stop planning our future." She turned back toward the kitchen, seeking the fortification only solid food could provide.

"You don't want kids?" he asked.

She rummaged, opening one cabinet then the next. "Whether I want kids or not is irrelevant."

"But—"

"I'm not going to marry you. We aren't going to have kids together."

"I don't understand. You don't want to get married?"

"No. I don't."

"But it's the perfect solution to our problems."

She abandoned her search for food and tore into him. "I don't want to be somebody's solution. Don't you get it?"

He stared at her somewhat blankly. "Get what?"

"Love. Marriage. Relationships. Don't you get it yet? Any of it? A wife isn't something you get at the pound like a dog. A wife isn't something you acquire or pick up on vacation."

An expression of dismay crossed his face and he stepped back, as if recoiling from her words. "I don't think of you that way."

"Yes, you do. You want to marry me because I'm convenient. And because then you'll get to help me— rescue me from financial despair. Not because you care about me."

"That's not—"

"Yes, it is. Two weeks ago, you couldn't have picked me out of a lineup. Before you walked through that door, you probably hadn't thought about me in a decade. Maybe more."

The expression on his face—shocked and maybe a little hurt—pulled at her heartstrings. Heartstrings that were already strung too tight.

She ached to reach out and touch him, but crossed her arms firmly over her chest instead. "Look, Brad, I'm sorry you feel lonely. And I'm sorry you don't want to be alone on your birthday. But marrying me wouldn't make that any better."

The color drained from his face and he sagged against the counter. "I thought you cared about me."

"Jeez, Brad, how can you be so smart about some things and not have a clue about others?"

He backed up a step, as if surprised by her vehemence.

"You think I don't care about you? Of course I care about you. I've been in love with you since I was eleven. But marrying you would be a disaster. Our marriage wouldn't last any longer than your marriage to Ginger did."

He opened his mouth, then closed it again, as if still confused, before saying, "So you don't love me anymore?"

She crossed the kitchen to stand before him. "No. You don't love me." When that did little to clarify his confusion, she went on. "I need to be loved. I can't marry you just to help you meet some goal. I deserve better than that. And you deserve better than a woman who would marry you for money."

She forced herself to meet his gaze, despite how hard it was. She needed him to believe her. She couldn't do this more than once. "You were worried about making the same mistakes you made with Ginger? Then don't make them. You may think you need me, but you don't."

"Damn it, Mattie, I'm not worried about that. I do need you."

"No, you don't. You'll be fine."

"Okay then. You need me. You said you never wanted to worry about money again. I can do that for you. I can help you pay off that damn loan. I can save your precious store. I can take you away from all this.

We can live in San Francisco. You can teach. We can go to Brazil. Whatever you want."

Despite herself, his words gave her pause, but only for a few seconds. "I need more than that. A few weeks, even a few days ago, that would have been enough. But you said it yourself. I deserve to be happy just as much as everyone else."

As she said the words, part of her started to believe they just might be true.

"Okay, so you won't marry me for money, but there's got to be something." He paced to the far end of the room, shoving his fingers through his hair in a way she found fascinating.

The dull ache that had been settling in her chest suddenly expanded. The pain gave her the courage and strength to be harsh. "Give it up, Brad. You're not going to win this one."

He turned, the intensity of his expression pinning her where she stood. The corners of his mouth tilted in a humorless smile. "Don't forget, Mattie. I never lose."

She felt a shiver of apprehension, but she dismissed it. He wasn't going to win. Not this time. Because she'd meant everything she'd said. She would never marry Brad, because he didn't love her.

Oh, he'd tempted her. Dear God, she practically ached to say yes. But in her mind and in her heart, she knew he'd only make her miserable. Far more miserable than giving up her dreams for other people had ever made her. She did deserve to be happy. And she deserved to be loved.

But he didn't love her. Nothing he could say or do would convince her he did.

17

"WHERE THE HELL is she?" The words were out of his mouth before the door even slammed shut behind him. The bell continued to jingle in the silence that followed his question.

For a moment, all three women—Edith, Abigail and Lucy—simply stared at him. Then the two older women spoke at once.

"What do you mean, where is she?" Edith demanded, hands fisted on her wide hips.

Abigail's brightly painted lips pursed in a frown. "Isn't she with you?"

Lucy's silence drew his attention. Even when he stared at her, she said nothing.

Edith scowled, seemingly unaware of Lucy's silence. "She hasn't missed a day in years. We assumed, since she wasn't here to open the store, that she was with you."

"She isn't."

"Oh, dear," Abigail murmured. "Our Mattie is missing."

Lucy—he noticed—showed no signs of concern. Silently she crept toward the door, apparently hoping to escape unnoticed.

"Now Abigail," Edith warned. "Don't leap to conclusions. Just because she isn't here doesn't mean she's missing. I'm sure Brad here can tell us what happened." She turned her steely glare in his direction. "Can't you?"

How the hell was he supposed to tell them what happened? He hardly knew himself. To him, it seemed like one minute he was having the best sex of his life and the next she was booting him out the door and telling him to go away. Somewhere in between he'd asked her to marry him. Since that seemed to be the moment everything went straight to hell, he started there.

"She and I had a—" he almost said fight, then thought better of it "—a disagreement. Yesterday morning." He wanted to leave it there, but the three women were all staring at him, waiting for him to continue, so he did. "She left to come to work, but she didn't come back."

Edith frowned. "She never came in. Thursday's her day off."

Brad digested that. "She worked last Thursday."

"She often does," Abigail said. "The hard worker harvests the most, after all."

"But with you in town, we didn't think anything of her not coming in yesterday." Edith's frown deepened. "But if she's not with you, then where is she?"

He raised an eyebrow. This would be almost amusing under other circumstances. As it was, he didn't have the patience to play Twenty Questions. "That's what I'm trying to find out."

He'd spent the past eighteen hours cursing himself for letting her leave. While he thought she was at work, he'd gone out to buy flowers.

Damn. What a pathetic sap he'd turned out to be. He'd spent hours visiting half the florist shops in town, searching for flowers that looked like the ones from his grandmother's yard and smelled like Mattie. He'd been so proud of himself for buying a vase of freesia—until late last night, when he realized she wasn't coming home. He'd never been so worried in his life.

Brad rammed his hands into his pockets and paced the length of the store. When he found himself facing an endless row of green fabric, he turned. "I just need to know she's all right."

Both Edith and Abigail remained silent, but after a moment, Lucy took a tiny step forward. "She's fine. She stayed with me last night. But don't even think about going over to my place or following me home or anything. She just wanted to be alone for a while."

Relief flooded through him. He saw his emotion mirrored in the eyes of Edith and Abigail. Then he saw it gradually replaced by suspicion.

"What exactly did you two 'disagree' about?"

He nearly winced at the censure in Edith's voice. Then he remembered that he'd done nothing wrong. He wasn't the bad guy here. "Hey, don't give me that look."

In his indignation, he was tempted to walk out then and there. He only wanted—needed—to talk to Mattie. He shouldn't have to defend himself to these three women first.

Yet common sense told him they were the gatekeepers here. If he didn't talk his way past them, he'd never get to Mattie. Hoping to placate them, he admitted, "I asked her to marry me."

"Hmm," Edith mumbled suspiciously.

"Oh, my," Abigail said, her clasped hands fidgeting. "And that upset her? That doesn't sound like Mattie. Are you sure she understood you?"

"Yes." He remembered the expression on Mattie's face as she told him she wouldn't marry him. "She understood me."

"Humph. You probably just didn't do it right. Men never get things right the first time." Edith's hands moved from her hips to cross under her massive bosom. "Well, you'd better tell us just what you told her and we'll see what we can do with it."

Before he could answer, Lucy rushed forward to stand in front of him, commandeering his sympathetic audience. "He doesn't really want to marry her. He doesn't love her. He just wants a wife and family and Mattie's convenient."

He tried to sidestep Lucy, but she put herself firmly in his path. "Of course I really want to marry her. I wouldn't have asked her to marry me if I didn't."

Lucy narrowed her eyes, assessing him with enough shrewd calculation to make him wonder how he'd ever mistaken her for an airhead. "Well," she said, "that still doesn't justify hurting Mattie the way you did."

"What exactly did I do that hurt Mattie?"

"You asked her to marry you."

"Yes." Maybe he was being an idiot here, but he still didn't see what was so wrong with that.

"You asked her for all the wrong reasons."

"All the wrong reasons? Is that what Mattie said?"

"She didn't have to say it. She told me what you said, how you asked her."

He considered her words for a moment. Could she be right? Was it possible that Mattie did want to marry him but that he'd just asked her the wrong way?

The thought eased some of the tightness in his chest. For the first time in nearly twenty-four hours, he felt he could breathe freely.

Okay, so maybe he hadn't lost her yet. Maybe he—

But common sense stopped him. Was he really willing to bet his future on the advice of a pregnant nineteen-year-old? He'd rather calculate his taxes on an abacus.

Shaking his head, he met Lucy's gaze. "Look, you're young and romantic." Her spine stiffened, so he added, "There's nothing wrong with that. But Mattie's practical. She wants financial security. I can offer her that."

The three women exchanged knowing looks.

"And that's what you told her?" Abigail asked doubtfully. "That's how you worded your proposal?"

"Yes, of course. We've both been married before. I presented arguments I knew would appeal to Mattie. Children, stability, financial security. Practical reasons."

"Practical reasons?" Edith snorted. "Damn foolish, if you ask me. Were you asking her to marry you or be your employee? Tell me something—you offer her a good 401K plan, too?"

Brad had to unclench his jaw before he could speak. "Mattie is a practical woman."

Edith snorted again. "Boy, after that proposal, you're lucky she didn't stone you."

"There was nothing wrong with my proposal. I offered her everything I have. My money, my fortune."

"Did you offer her your heart?" Edith said.

"My heart?"

"Yes, your heart." Lucy looked at him as if he was an idiot. "She doesn't want your money. She wants your love."

"You do love her, don't you?" Abigail asked.

Brad broke off, unsure of what to say. He turned, paced the length of the room then turned back. He eyed the three women cautiously before ramming his hands back into his pockets and staring aimlessly at a bolt of moss-green fabric.

He thought back to what Mattie had said that day about people seeing more shades of green than any other color. At the time, he'd thought she was exaggerating. Funny thing was, when he looked at that wall of fabric, he knew which bolt was exactly the shade of her eyes.

"Of course I love her."

"Did you tell her that?"

No, he hadn't told her. Why not? Why hadn't he seen it?

Because he'd wanted so badly to win. Somehow, he'd started thinking of his relationship with Mattie as a game. A competition. Hell, Ginger always said he was at his worst when he got competitive. In this case, it seemed she was right. He was so focused on winning, he didn't stop to think of what Mattie would want. He'd only been thinking about what he wanted.

He'd wanted it all. Wealth, success and a loving family. A home. Until Ginger walked out on him, it had never occurred to him that he might not be able to have both. That one might preclude the other.

Now he wasn't so sure. It was easy to blame his divorce on Ginger, but wasn't he to blame also? Had he really loved her enough? Or had he always put his needs first? His thirst for financial success before his marriage?

It was pointless to try to place blame now. All he knew was that he wasn't about to make the same mistakes twice. Financial success had not bought him his father's love. Now the only person whose love he really needed was Mattie's.

Yes, Mattie was practical. But she was also fun and playful. She didn't need someone to rescue her, she needed someone to play with. A playmate. Just like he did.

God, she was right. He really didn't know a thing about women.

Sighing, he pulled his hands from his pockets and rubbed them both down his face. He turned to face the women again.

"Damn, I am such an idiot." He let his hands drop to his sides and met Edith's gaze.

"Humph." But her expression softened slightly. "Men usually are."

"But not always," Lucy corrected with surprising conviction.

"No, not always," Abigail said.

"So you'll tell me where she is?" he asked Lucy. An unexpected urgency was driving him to find her, to tell her how he felt now, while it was still so new to him.

The girl considered it for only a moment before shaking her head. "No. You screwed up. You need to figure out how to fix this or you'll just end up hurting her again."

"Damn it, how am I supposed to do that?"

The corners of Lucy's mouth tilted upward in a mysterious little smile. "You'll think of something."

"Oh, yes," Abigail added. "Only the strongest men can scale the obstacles in the path to a woman's heart."

"Don't be daft, boy," Edith chimed in. "She spent the last week teaching you how to understand women. Surely you learned something useful."

18

LOSING BRAD at twenty-one, when she'd never really had him, was devastating. Losing Brad at twenty-nine after lying in his arms, sleeping by his side and making love to him long into the night? There were simply no words for it.

She wondered why the Nobel committee gave out awards for simple things like medical research and promoting world peace, but ignored the efforts of the brokenhearted to keep stumbling along as if nothing was wrong.

Worst of all, she couldn't talk about her heartache with anyone. Jessica called every few days, but their conversations were brief. Mattie answered Jess's questions about "how it had gone with Brad" as quickly as possible then changed the subject. Jessica—half a world away—would only worry if she knew how Mattie felt.

Edith, Abigail and Lucy tried to be supportive and understanding. But she didn't want to burden them. So for their sake, she insisted—repeatedly—that she was fine, relieved even to have the house back to herself, but she didn't think they believed her.

For days they tiptoed around the store, looking just as solemn and sad as she felt. Then one by one, their attitudes changed. Twice she caught them whispering conspiratorially to each other, only to break apart when she walked by. They smiled nonchalantly at her, then winked at each other when they thought she wasn't looking.

Oh, they were definitely up to something. She could muster only enough emotion to hope it wasn't a repeat of the disastrous matchmaking they'd attempted after her divorce. Edith's nephew was perfectly nice, but she simply wasn't interested in a man who had six children, she didn't care how great his health issuance was through the Pac-N-Sac.

Mostly she stayed at the store, locking herself in her office or in the inventory room upstairs where she could pretend to work, away from prying eyes. Which is where Lucy found her, over a week after Brad had left, sorting and pricing bolts of fabric.

First she heard the heavy footfall of a pregnant woman lumbering up too many stairs. Shaking her head in exasperation, she dusted off her hands and rose from her knees. She crossed to the door at the back of the room, which led to the flight of stairs. Before she could throw open the door and chastise Lucy, the girl slipped into the room and nudged the door shut behind her.

Propping her hands on her hips, she scolded the girl. "The doctor said you should be taking it easy. Climbing up—"

Lucy held up a hand, cutting her off mid-rant. "Someone's here to see the owner."

For an instant, her mouth hung open. Then she

snapped it closed. Making another attempt to dust off her hands, she said, "Well, obviously, I can't see anyone like this. They'll have to make an appointment and come back tomorrow." Then her curiosity got the better of her and she asked, "Did they say what they want?"

Lucy smiled sheepishly. "It's someone who wants to rent this space."

"Oh." She'd dressed to do inventory, not to meet a potential tenant. Still, if she turned this person away, he or she might not come back. "Well, then show them in."

Lucy's smile broadened, but instead of heading to the door, she hurried to Mattie's side. With maternal ease, she smoothed Mattie's hair and tucked a strand behind her ear.

Mattie swatted her hands away. "Lucy. I'm sure it's fine for...whoever this is."

Lucy shrugged impishly, then bustled out, leaving the door open behind her. Before Mattie could decide if Lucy was up to something or merely hopped up on pregnancy hormones, the door swung open and Brad stepped into the room.

Mattie inhaled sharply, pulling in enough dust to choke an elephant. She sputtered, coughed, then wished she could simply disappear into thin air rather than face the humiliation of fending off her employees' matchmaking. And she knew how she must look to him. Knew dust streaked her sweatshirt and the knees of her jeans. Knew her hair hung about her face in a tangled mess, despite Lucy's efforts.

It certainly didn't help matters that he looked so damn good it made her heart ache. He wore jeans and a plaid, long-sleeved shirt. He looked comfortable. Simple. Unpretentious.

And it was all she could do not to throw herself across the room and into his arms. Somehow she stood firm.

"Why are you here?" Her voice sounded hoarse. From the dust. Yeah, that was it.

He stepped farther into the room and closed the door behind him. "I'm here to talk to you about leasing this space."

"Stop wasting my time." She turned her back to him and picked up her clipboard. *Let him think you're too busy to talk to him.*

"I'm not." He waited until she'd turned to face him again. "I called last week and got all the details from Edith. I'll sign the lease right now. I can write you checks for the first and last month's rent."

She didn't bother to hide her suspicion. "What is this, Brad? Just another tactic? You still looking to win?"

He shook his head. "You told me I couldn't win this one. You were right."

The glimmer of honesty in his eyes surprised her. "Then what are you doing here?"

"Just what I said. I want to rent this office space."

"You have an office in San Francisco."

"I *had* an office in San Francisco. I canceled my lease. I decided it was time I moved home. Until I came back, I never realized how much I missed being here."

His tone was filled with yearning. It wasn't hard for her to believe that he wanted to move back home. After all, she'd lived here nearly all her life. This town was a part of her. Why wouldn't it be a part of him?

But to lease him the space in her building? See him every day? How could she do that?

He must have sensed her waffling, because he moved toward her, his voice soothing and persuasive. "I know you could use the income from the lease. The monthly rent will more than cover the business loan you're paying off. And I'll be nearby. I can help out, whenever I'm needed."

He stopped just inches away. For a moment, time stood still. Light streamed in through the floor-to-ceiling windows. The sunshine highlighted the blond in his hair and brightened the blue of his eyes. Even the dust motes floating through the air seemed to vibrate with the energy flowing between them. He reached out and brushed his knuckles against her cheek.

She forced herself to step away from his touch, but she moved slowly, as if battling the will of her own body.

"No, Brad. I can't do this. You just keep pushing and pushing." Her voice rose sharply, sounded panicked and overwrought even to her own ears. "I don't want—"

He pulled her into his arms, cradling her head against his shoulder. "Shh. It's okay."

She relaxed against him, feeling safe within the strength of his embrace. She inhaled deeply. The spicy scent of his cologne mixed with the fresh scent of his soap and the faint scent of dust still in the air. The combination washed over her, easing the tension that had been building within her.

Rocking her gently back and forth, he murmured. "I'm not going to push you anymore."

Her muscles tightened with surprise. She pulled away from him. "You've changed your mind?"

He loosened his arms, holding her just far enough away from him to look steadily into her eyes. "No. I haven't changed my mind. I still want to marry you. I love you."

Her heart leaped in her chest then thudded against her rib cage. "You—"

"Let me finish." He pressed a finger against her lips. "When I asked you to marry me, I offered you everything I thought a woman would want. But I didn't think about what you would want."

He cradled her face in his palm, gently stroking her cheek with his thumb. Emotion tore through her. She wanted to throw her arms around his neck and say yes. Yet even more, she wanted to hear what he had to say.

"All your life, you've made sacrifices for other people. You gave up your dream of joining the Peace Corps for Mike. You gave up your teaching career for your grandmother. I don't want to be another person you make sacrifices for. I want to be the one who makes sacrifices for you."

"I don't understand."

"All my life, I've known what I wanted. Money, a business, a marriage, kids. Now, all I want is to be with you. If I can't have you, then I don't want to be married. The only thing I want more than to marry you is to know you're happy."

He stepped away from her, pressing a fat envelope into her hand.

The envelope bore the logo of a local travel agency. She thumbed open the flap, then withdrew the stack of papers inside. There were several folded sheets of paper, but the bulk of the contents was a packet of airline vouchers.

Staring at the papers, she read aloud the destination. "Rio de Janeiro. Brazil. You're giving me tickets to Brazil?"

"It's not the Peace Corps, but..." He shrugged. "Apparently, the application process is pretty complicated. And you don't get to choose where you go. Hopefully, this is almost as good. There's a research station in the Brazilian rain forest that needs an elementary teacher for the children of the scientists. It's a two-year job, starting in September. You would leave next week for Rio for a six-week crash course in Portuguese."

Overwhelmed by the magnitude of the gift, she could do no more than stare numbly at the tickets. Slowly shaking her head, she muttered, "I can't leave—"

Again he cut her off. "I knew you wouldn't want to leave the store. That's why I'm moving back to Palo Verde. I'll be right here. Edith and Abigail swear they can run the store on their own. Lucy is going to start business classes at the community college in the spring. She's already studying for the GED. By the time you get back from Brazil, she'll be ready to take over the store. You can go back to teaching. Or you can travel. Whatever you want.''

Still reeling, she stepped away from him to sit on a stack of boxes. ''So this is what they were up to. I knew they were plotting something. But I...'' Her voice trailed off. ''I can't believe you've done this.'' She looked up at him, not bothering to blink back the tears pooling in her eyes. ''What about your business? You said it was the most important thing in your life. But managing a quilt shop on the side would take so much time. And if you do this, you're giving up your goal of having a family.''

He knelt before her, going down on one knee as if proposing. ''Mattie, those goals I set for myself were things I thought would make me happy. They were things I thought would earn me respect and make me a man. Then I fell in love with you. Now the only person's respect I want is yours. The only man I want to be is the man who makes you happy.''

''And you would give up everything for that?''

''In a minute.''

Barely able to believe him but willing to trust, she set the plane tickets aside and took his face in her hands. ''Oh, Brad, you wonderful crazy man! I don't want to join the Peace Corps. I don't want to go live in Brazil.''

''But it's what you've always wanted.''

''You're what I've always wanted. I want a life with you. Here. Anywhere you want to live. Yes, I used to fantasize about doing all those things, but I wouldn't want to do them without you. If we weren't together, what would be the point?''

Words seemed inadequate, so she lowered her mouth to his and kissed him, pouring her whole heart and her whole soul into the kiss. His mouth moved with hers, welcoming her, warming her heart and her body.

He deepened the kiss, snaking his hand to the back of her head. The other arm pulled her to him. She scooted off the box to kneel beside him on the floor. Plastering her body against his, she wrapped her arms around his waist to hold him close.

He kissed her as if he never wanted to stop, as if he simply couldn't get enough of her. As if he could spend the rest of his life kissing her.

And for the first time, she believed it. No longer afraid of having her heart crushed by him or of losing herself in her desire to be with him, she poured her whole heart into the kiss.

When he finally pulled back, they were both gasping for breath. He pressed his forehead to hers. With his eyes still closed and his hand still cupping the back of her head, he waited for their breathing to slow. Then he leaned back just enough to meet her eyes and asked, "Does this mean you won't be taking the position in Brazil?"

She laughed, partly out of joy, partly out of disbelief. "No. I won't be going to Brazil. I don't want to go anywhere without you."

His eyes closed in relief. "Thank God."

She pulled back further to study him. "You didn't really think I'd go, did you?"

"I hoped you wouldn't," he admitted sheepishly.

"But I would have let you. It damn near would have killed me, but I would have let you."

She kissed him again, testing his resolve. "You knew I'd stay," she teased him.

"I hoped. I didn't know." He stood, helping her to her feet as he did. "Since you're not going to be working in Brazil for the next two years, how would you like to go there for our honeymoon?"

Interlacing their fingers, she clasped his hand. "You know, I still haven't agreed to marry you." A pained looked crossed his face. "But—" she hastily reassured him "—a honeymoon in Brazil sounds perfect. Just perfect."

She'd been so sure there was nothing he could do that would convince her he loved her. How wrong she'd been.

She'd tried so hard to defend her heart against him. Only now did she realize how pointless it had been to try to keep him out of her heart. He'd been there all along.

__Epilogue__

"You know, when I asked you to look out for my brother while I was gone, I didn't mean you had to do it forever."

Mattie looked at her best friend—now her sister-in-law—and smiled. "Well, I did promise. And you know how seriously I take promises."

There was a glimmer of sorrow in Jessica's eyes as she raised her champagne glass in a silent toast. For an instant, Mattie wondered if there was something going on in Jessica's life that her friend hadn't told her about. Then the moment passed, and Jessica said, with mock solemnity, "Thank you for making my brother happy."

"Trust me, I've been waiting a long time for this."

"You know, he always did want to be part of your family."

"Watch it, I might start to worry that he married me just for that," she teased, even though she didn't really believe it.

But looking out across her father's lawn, she could see why. Brad's parents—who'd nearly had a fit when she insisted on holding the reception in her father's backyard rather than the country club—sat quietly at one of the tables. They looked out of place and unhappy. Not enough rich and influential people on the guest list, she suspected.

Her father, on the other hand, had spent most of the afternoon playing with the children on the front lawn. Even now, he was trying to coax Brad into playing. After a few minutes of conversation, Brad handed newborn Hannah back to Lucy, then jogged over to where Jessica and Mattie sat on the back porch.

The reception had been going on for hours, and both she and Brad had long ago changed out of their wedding clothes and into jeans. They were leaving for Sacramento in a few hours where they'd stay overnight before catching an early flight to Brazil the next day.

Brad crouched down beside her chair. "Your father's putting together a game of flag football. What do you say?"

Flag football on her wedding day? She almost laughed, it was so preposterous. Then she saw the challenging glint in his blue eyes.

This man had given her everything she'd ever wanted. He'd fulfilled her every dream. Her grandmother's quilt shop was now being run—for the most part—by Edith, Abigail and Lucy. In just a few weeks, she'd be taking over for one of the middle-school teachers who was starting maternity leave. And though she couldn't wait to get back in the classroom, she was happy knowing that the quilt store would be well run and financially solvent, thanks to the extra money brought in by Brad's rent.

And yet all of that was superfluous to the sheer joy she felt when she was with him. He'd made her so happy. How could she say no to him? Why would she even want to?

She sat forward, bracing her elbows on her knees. "So tell me, now that we're married, are you finally gonna pick me to be on your team?"

He grinned. "Why would I do that?"

"That's what I thought." She reached out and pulled off his Titleist baseball cap. As she stood, she put the hat on her own head and pulled her hair into a stubby ponytail that hung out the back.

Brad groaned and lunged for her. She darted out of his reach, only to let him catch her moments later. He pulled her close to his chest, one arm around her shoulders, the other at her hips. "What am I going to do with you, Sprout?"

She planted a quick kiss on his lips before replying. "I'll tell you what you're not going to do."

"What's that?"

"You're not going to beat me at flag football." She pulled away from him, tugging at his hand as she headed for the front lawn.

"I don't need to. I've already won."

Single in South Beach

Nightlife on the Strip just got a little hotter!

Join author Joanne Rock as she takes you back to Miami Beach and its hottest singles' playground. Club Paradise has staked its claim in the decadent South Beach nightlife and the women in charge are determined to keep the sexy resort on top. So what will they do with the hot men who show up at the club?

GIRL GONE WILD
Harlequin Blaze #135
May 2004

DATE WITH A DIVA
Harlequin Blaze #139
June 2004

HER FINAL FLING
Harlequin Temptation #983
July 2004

Don't miss the continuation of this red-hot series from Joanne Rock!

Look for these books at your favorite retail outlet.

If you enjoyed what you just read,
then we've got an offer you can't resist!

Take 2 bestselling
love stories FREE!
Plus get a FREE surprise gift!

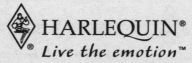

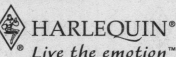